Praise for the novels of Cassie Edwards

"High adventure and a surprise season this Indian romance." —*Affaire de Coeur*

"Edwards puts an emphasis on placing authentic customs and language in each book. Her Indian books have generated much interest throughout the country, and elsewhere." —*Journal-Gazette* (Mattoon, IL)

"Few can relate a story as well as Ms. Edwards." —*Midwest Book Review*

"Edwards consistently gives the reader a strong love story, rich in Indian lore, filled with passion and memorable characters." —*Romantic Times*

"Excellent . . . an endearing story . . . filled with heart-warming characters." —Under the Covers

"A fine writer . . . accurate. . . . Indian history and language keep readers interested." —*Tribune* (Greeley, CO)

"Captivating . . . heartwarming . . . beautiful . . . a winner." —*Rendezvous*

"Edwards moves readers with love and compassion." —*Bell, Book & Candle*

SILVER FEATHER

Cassie Edwards

A SIGNET BOOK

SIGNET
Published by New American Library, a division of
Penguin Group (USA) Inc., 375 Hudson Street,
New York, New York 10014, USA
Penguin Group (Canada), 10 Alcorn Avenue, Toronto,
Ontario M4V 3B2, Canada (a division of Pearson Penguin Canada Inc.)
Penguin Books Ltd., 80 Strand, London WC2R 0RL, England
Penguin Ireland, 25 St. Stephen's Green, Dublin 2,
Ireland (a division of Penguin Books Ltd.)
Penguin Group (Australia), 250 Camberwell Road, Camberwell, Victoria 3124,
Australia (a division of Pearson Australia Group Pty. Ltd.)
Penguin Books India Pvt. Ltd., 11 Community Centre, Panchsheel Park,
New Delhi - 110 017, India
Penguin Group (NZ), cnr Airborne and Rosedale Roads, Albany,
Auckland 1310, New Zealand (a division of Pearson New Zealand Ltd.)
Penguin Books (South Africa) (Pty.) Ltd., 24 Sturdee Avenue,
Rosebank, Johannesburg 2196, South Africa

Penguin Books Ltd., Registered Offices:
80 Strand, London WC2R 0RL, England

First published by Signet, an imprint of New American Library,
a division of Penguin Group (USA) Inc.

First Printing, June 2005
10 9 8 7 6 5 4 3 2 1

They came from a faraway land, as they
walked to a place that is not so grand.
They fought with all their might,
but in the end, there was no light.
Their heads always held high,
but now a tear in their eye.
They always chanted and sang their songs,
but now they don't understand what they did wrong.
Their souls were always filled with happiness,
but now they are filled with great sadness.
It was a long journey, this I know,
But to the American Indian . . . they did grow.

—Shelly Jackson,
a fan, friend, and poet

Chapter 1

Innocent is the heart's devotion,
With which I worship thine.
            —Percy Bysshe Shelley

The Mississippi Valley Region—1814
Wee-pah-zoo-kah-wee . . . Juneberry Moon

"Come on, Silver Feather," Diana said as she yanked on his hand. They ran down the cold, dark space of a secret passageway in Dettro Manor, Diana's stepfather's huge plantation house. "I've already prepared a place where we can eat our cookies and talk. But we must hurry, Silver Feather. Should your absence be discovered . . ."

"Do not worry so much about things," Silver Feather said as he looked over at Diana. Her golden hair shone like silk beneath the dim light of the lantern that he was carrying.

She was so exquisitely pretty. He remembered that the first time he had seen her, she had taken his breath away. Today she was petite and looked lovely in her dress with its skirt that billowed out from her tiny waist. Her lashes were thick, and her eyes were the color of the sky.

"The cookies smell good," he continued. "It is making my belly growl. Do you hear it?"

"Yes, I hear it," Diana said, giggling. "My belly is growling, too."

Enjoying their stolen time together, Diana peeked at him. As usual, he wore a full outfit of buckskin, with thick fringes along the sleeves of his shirt. His raven-black hair was worn long and loose down his back. His fringed buckskin moccasins barely made a sound as he walked.

Silver Feather gladly followed Diana. Too soon he would have to return to the real world, a world that was sad and demeaning to his Choctaw mother and father, and to their clan as a whole!

Silver Feather was fourteen winters of age, Diana was ten.

Diana's stepfather had cheated Silver Feather's Choctaw Eagle Clan, then forced them to labor for him.

They had no choice but to live on the plantation grounds, and the land that had once been theirs now belonged to Jamieson Dettro, a retired colonel from the United States military.

"Here, Silver Feather. This is a wonderful place to enjoy the cookies," Diana said, dropping her hand from his. "I've spread Mama's pretty patchwork quilt for us. I adore it. Before Mama died, she made this quilt from her beautiful velveteen dresses that she no longer wore."

Silver Feather held the lantern low enough to see the colorful squares that had been sewn together to make the quilt. The patches were all shades of purple, blue, red, and green. He bent to a knee and ran his hand over the soft fabric, then smiled up at Diana.

"It feels like your skin, Diana. So soft," he said, drawing more giggles from her.

"No, it feels more like yours," she said. "I love to touch your copper skin. It has the texture of velvet."

She set her bundle of cookies down on the quilt, then patted a place next to her. "Please, sit."

Silver Feather plopped down beside her, then placed the lantern on the floor in front of them. His eyes widened as she unfolded the cloth and spread it out, revealing the luscious-smelling cookies.

"Take one," Diana said. "Priscilla, my maid, made these especially for us, Silver Feather."

"Then she knows about our times together here in the secret passageways?" Silver Feather asked guardedly as he plucked up one of the cookies.

He eagerly took a bite, then closed his eyes as he enjoyed the sweetness.

Diana nodded as she took a cookie for herself. "She knows we meet secretly, but she doesn't know *where* we meet. My stepfather doesn't even know the passageways exist, or he'd surely have talked about it to me. He bought this mansion from a slave trader a few years ago."

She gave Silver Feather a serious look. "I promised that I'd never tell anyone about the passageways," she said. "That means nobody, Silver Feather. Absolutely nobody. Especially not Priscilla. She's black and belongs to my stepfather. You know how he gets information from those he owns."

"Yes, I have seen it too often," Silver Feather said, nodding slowly. "I fear him taking his whip to my father or mother. He has threatened, but he has yet to do it."

He lowered his eyes. "He has whipped some of my friends' parents, though," he said, his voice breaking. "He whips them until their backs become raw and bloody."

"I know," Diana murmured. She reached out a tiny hand and touched his arm. "And I'm so sorry. I wish there was something I could do. You and your people are treated terribly."

"Colonel Dettro stole my people's land. One day I hope to prove it and set my people free," Silver Feather said. "Now, though, they must work days and spend their nights in the ramshackle shacks behind Dettro Manor."

He placed the half-eaten cookie on the quilt beside him. Suddenly he wasn't so hungry after all.

Instead, he felt guilty for being with Diana, away from the grueling work of picking cotton, while everyone else of his clan was sweating away beneath the hot sun.

But he just could not ignore the opportunity to be with Diana. It was not to get out of work. It was to be with her. She had brought so much into his life.

He knew that others considered them too young to be in love, but he knew that he loved Diana and would for the rest of his life.

"I miss my parents so much," Diana said, her voice breaking. She set her own uneaten cookie aside. "Papa died during a fierce battle when I was barely old enough to remember his face. Mama married Colonel Dettro a short time after, mainly to have a place where she could raise me. And then . . . and then . . . just last year Mama passed away. It was her heart."

"And so now you live alone with your stepfather," Silver Feather said, gently taking one of her hands. "You said that he has never been cruel to you. But how could anyone be? You are all sweetness, Diana."

Diana blushed and lowered her eyes, then gazed up at him again and smiled, reveling in the touch of his hand in hers. "I just read a beautiful story about a mythical goddess. She was called Diana, Goddess of the Hunt. I will grow up and be a huntress. When I am your wife, I will join you on your hunts, and I will be *your* Goddess of the Hunt."

"One must be free first to be able to go on hunts," Silver Feather said sadly. He slid his hand out of hers. "I dream, Diana, of when I hunted with my father, before we lost everything. I dream of riding a white stallion, its mane shining like your hair. I dream that the horse is mine."

"Silver Feather, one day you will be free of my stepfather, and you will be a great Choctaw chief of your Eagle Clan, with your own village and warriors. You will own such a steed. And . . . I will be your wife," Diana murmured.

She closed her eyes. "I see myself standing beside you and holding a bouquet of bluebells on our wedding day," she said softly.

Her eyes opened.

"Bluebells were my mama's favorite flower, you know," she said, a sob catching in her throat. "I loved gathering bluebells with her on our walks in the forest. It seems so long ago."

Silver Feather reached over and placed a finger beneath her chin and slowly lifted it. Their eyes met.

"Diana, I promise you bluebells on our wedding day," he said. He smiled into her eyes, then dropped his hand and turned his head away almost as quickly. "But the truth is, I doubt that any of that can ever happen. My Choctaw clan is doomed."

He swallowed hard and ran a hand through his long black hair.

"My father is chief of our clan. He tried to use trade to bolster his authority and prestige, but in truth his standing was lessened after he was cheated, and then he lost his land and freedom because of it," he said angrily.

"But how could your father let that happen?" Diana asked, aching at seeing Silver Feather tortured by these past deeds. "He is your father. You are intelligent. Surely he is, as well."

Silver Feather rested his hands on his lap.

"What happened to my father has happened to so many like him. They are intelligent men, but they cannot read the white man's language. It is a common tactic used by whites. They use it to bankrupt Indians. My father says it is called the Indian Factory System."

"You have never spoken of this to me before," Diana said. "What is the Indian Factory System?"

"In the beginning, it was meant to help both Indians and whites alike, but it changed into something ugly," he said with the maturity of an adult. "Trading posts called factories were established by the United States government among the Indians to provide needed goods and to prevent exploitation by unscrupulous traders."

"And that wasn't what happened?" Diana asked, interested in this new information.

"For a while," Silver Feather said. "But my father said that the system was manipulated and corrupted. Indians were encouraged to incur ex-

cessive debts at the trading posts—so large that
they could not be repaid. That is why tribes like
the Choctaw were forced to work for plantation
owners, to cancel their debts."

"And that is why your people are here," Diana
murmured. "I'm so sorry."

"That is not the whole reason," Silver Feather
said. "Your stepfather bribed my father into getting his supplies from him instead of at the trading
post. Then your stepfather raised the prices."

A sound in the passageway made Silver Feather
and Diana both gasp with fear.

"What if it's my stepfather?" Diana whispered,
grabbing Silver Feather's arm.

They both sighed with relief and laughed when
a hefty rat came sniffing around.

Diana took one of the cookies and pitched it as
far as she could down the passageway, and the rat
scrambled after it.

"We'd best go, don't you think?" she said, looking solemnly at the untouched cookies and then at
Silver Feather.

"Yes, my absence might be noticed if I stay
much longer," Silver Feather said.

"We didn't eat the cookies," Diana said, disap-
pointment shining in her eyes. "I shall bring some
again soon."

"We can always just sit and be together," Silver
Feather said. "That is enough for me."

He watched her shake the cookies out of the

napkin for the rat. Silver Feather would have liked to take them home, but he knew that would only bring unwanted attention to him. His mother would want to know how he had acquired the cookies, which could reveal his private moments with his Diana. He would never chance that, not for anything.

Diana folded the quilt and placed it in a small chest that she had brought from the attic to store items for these clandestine meetings. Then they ran through the long passageway until they saw light ahead of them.

The underground passageways began far away from the cotton field, and the opening was hidden beneath thick brush. Diana had just happened upon it one day when she had chased a rabbit into the brush. The rabbit disappeared into the tunnel she had so innocently uncovered. Not long after that, she shared her discovery with Silver Feather, and since then, they had been meeting there often.

"I shall see you soon, Silver Feather," Diana said as she ran on her way.

Silver Feather watched her until she was out of sight, then ran toward the cabins in the distance himself.

The sun was just sinking in the sky, which meant that by now his mother would already be home, beginning the evening meal in the small fireplace.

He believed that his father was meeting with the others who once had been powerful warriors.

Huffing and puffing from running so hard past the empty cotton fields, Silver Feather finally reached his cabin.

He hurried inside and found his mother preparing their scanty meal of corn harvested from their family's private corn patch, along with whatever edible greens she had found in the nearby forest.

The smell was the same each evening, since that was the only food they had.

"Son, you have been with Diana again, have you not?" Morning Snow asked. She groaned as she straightened up from a stooped position on the scratched old oak floor.

Her doeskin dress, which at one time had been spotlessly white, was now soiled and yellowed. She wore her hair in one long braid down her back, and her dark eyes showed her weariness.

"Son, being with Diana is going to get our whole clan in trouble. Please be careful. Although we have lost so much, we at least still have food, clothes, and lodging."

"Mother, one day I will live as I am supposed to live," Silver Feather said, lifting his chin proudly. "I am going to be a powerful chief, and Diana is going to be my wife. She is going to be my Goddess of the Hunt."

"Goddess of the Hunt?" Morning Snow

snapped back at him. "Son, son, what has that pretty little thing put in your mind today?"

Morning Snow went to Silver Feather and drew him gently into her arms.

"My son, you can have your dreams," she murmured. "Sometimes they are all that keep me alive."

"I wish I could do more than dream," Silver Feather said, easing from her arms. "I wish that you could have more than your dreams."

"Who is speaking of dreams?"

At the voice of Silver Feather's father, the boy turned to see him coming through the door.

He was a tall, powerfully built man, yet now he stooped when he walked, as though the white landowner had beaten him down.

"It is nothing," Morning Snow said as she went to give her husband a hug. "It is just our son talking of things that will never come to pass."

His father, Silent Arrow, patted his wife gently on the back, then stepped away from her to the fireplace, watching the flames lapping at the logs.

"If only I could find those papers," he said. He turned to his wife. "If I could find the papers that Colonel Dettro has in that big house of his, I could prove how he cheated our Choctaw clan."

Silver Feather's eyes widened at the mention of the papers' being in the Dettro mansion. His heart pounded as he thought about the secret passageways that led to many rooms of the mansion. If he could somehow get into those rooms and find those papers, everything in his people's lives could change!

He could hardly wait to see Diana again so that he could tell her about his plan.

He would find a way to right all the wrongs done to his Eagle Clan!

Chapter 2

Love pour'd her beauty
Into my warm veins.
— John Keats

The sun was scalding hot as Silver Feather plucked first one fluffy white boll of cotton from its stem, then another and another.

He gazed over at his mother, whose back seemed more bent today than yesterday as she continued picking cotton alongside her husband.

It hurt him deeply to see how red and raw her fingertips were.

Silver Feather was glad to see the sun lowered to the point in the sky where he knew that it was almost time to stop for the day.

He glanced over his shoulder at the other people of his clan—men, women, and children—in the cotton field. Their sweat-soaked buckskins were clinging to their bodies, and their coal-black hair hung in wet strings down their backs.

"I do not think I can go another step," his

mother said as she stopped to press a hand to the small of her back.

She groaned, trying to stretch the pain away.

"You must," Silent Arrow told her, nodding toward the overseer, Frank Owens, who for the moment was looking elsewhere. They could see Frank's black whip, coiled and ready to snap across someone's back.

"Yes, I know," Morning Snow said, sighing.

She went back to picking cotton, and Silver Feather followed behind her and his father.

Finally, the moment everyone had been waiting for arrived. A gun fired into the air, signaling the slave laborers that it was time to collect their bags of cotton and bring them in for weighing.

Morning Snow sighed again, then tried to lift the heavy bag of cotton.

"Mother, I will carry yours as well as mine," Silver Feather said, reaching out to take her bag.

She yanked it back from him, fear in her weary eyes. "No," she said quickly. "I will be punished if I do not carry my own. Son, just tend to yours. It is heavy enough for such a child to carry."

"Mother, I am no longer a child," Silver Feather corrected. "I am a man."

His mother gave a rare smile.

"Yes, you are a man," Morning Snow said, then dragged her bulging bag of cotton behind her as her husband and son lifted theirs and slung them over their shoulders. "This hard life has stolen your childhood away from you. You are, indeed, a man walking in the shoes of a child."

Silver Feather smiled proudly at his mother. He was strong and quick. And he picked as much cotton as most people who were twice his age.

They walked toward the shed where the others were already standing in line waiting to have their bags weighed. Silver Feather's stomach tensed when he got in line with his mother and father. He watched Colonel Dettro, who stood just outside the shed, recording in his ledger how many pounds had been picked by each individual.

If the colonel saw that someone didn't pick enough cotton, he would send that person back out into the field to pick more. If the worker still did not reach the quota, he or she was made to stay in the fields, alone, for the rest of the night. As morning came and the others returned to the fields, the person would have to stay out in the fields and begin all over again, filling a new bag that would be weighed for that day.

It was something everyone tried to guard against.

"Quit your daydreamin', lad," Colonel Dettro said, jolting Silver Feather from his deep thoughts.

Silver Feather realized then that his mother and father were already in the shed.

He hurried to go inside, but just as he reached the door he saw something that turned his heart cold.

His father was attempting to fool with the scales in order to tip the balance of the weight of his wife's cotton in her favor so that she would not have to work at night, when she so badly needed that time to rest. If he was caught, he would be unmercifully whipped.

"Out of the way, lad," Colonel Dettro said, roughly shoving Silver Feather aside as he stepped into the shed just in time to see what Silver Feather's father was doing.

Silver Feather felt the blood drain from his face when the colonel yanked his pistol from its holster.

"You rascal dog!" Colonel Dettro shouted at Silver Feather's father. "How dare you tamper with my scales! You are nothing but a cheat!"

Silver Feather stumbled backward. He watched as the colonel raised his pistol and methodically shot Silver Feather's father in the belly, and then shot his mother.

For a moment Silver Feather could only stand and stare at his dead parents.

Then, afraid that he would be next, Silver Feather bolted outside into the cotton field.

He hunkered low so that neither the colonel nor any of his men could see him. Stooped over, he ran and ran, managing to elude Dettro's men, who were chasing him and calling his name.

Knowing that to stop could mean his death, Silver Feather ran onward until his side ached so much he could not go any farther.

Thankfully he was far enough from the fields and the mansion now to feel safe, so he stopped.

He struggled to catch his breath, and when he finally managed the feat, he crumpled to the ground and sobbed uncontrollably. He cried so much that he did not think that he could ever stop.

His heart was breaking. His whole world had been turned upside down. His beloved parents' breaths had been snuffed out as he watched.

"Why?" he cried to the heavens as he gazed into the fluffy white clouds overhead. "How could he have done this? How?"

A lone eagle suddenly appeared, soaring out from behind the clouds. It was so beautiful and peaceful, with its wide spread of wings. It swept lower and seemed to make eye contact with Silver Feather.

Silver Feather swallowed hard. He watched the bird, feeling something mystical, feeling that the eagle was trying to communicate with him.

And then it came to him. He remembered his father's teachings.

His father had often told him to be brave, bold, and proud, under all circumstances.

"Even this?" he cried, again to the heavens. "Father! Mother! How can you be gone from me? How could the white man be this heartless?"

He no longer saw the eagle, but instead the image of his father against the clouds.

Silver Feather remembered how proudly his father had held his head high, even in the worst of circumstances.

"Father, I, too, shall be strong!" he yelled to his father's image as it faded away, satisfied.

Silver Feather wiped at his eyes as he stared heavenward. Feeling blessed, he rose shakily to his feet.

"Father, I will make you proud of me. I promise," he said, this time more softly, but still with much emotion.

His jaw tight, his tears dried, Silver Feather searched for a place to hide. He wasn't sure what was to become of him now.

But there was one thing that kept running through his mind. The papers that his father had said could set his Eagle Clan free.

If Silver Feather could get into the house and find those papers, he would be a hero. But he would do it in honor of his beloved chieftain father, not himself.

But how? If he got anywhere near the plantation now, he might be the next to die.

Suddenly his heart leaped inside his chest. He heard the sound of a horse's hooves quickly approaching his hiding place. Trembling, his throat dry from fear, he knelt behind a thick stand of brush.

His pulse raced. He knew the horse was close enough that if he peeked through the brush, he would be able to see the rider.

Daringly, he parted some leaves and stems. His eyes widened with relief and excitement when he saw Diana on her pony. And she was alone.

His heart ached when he saw that she was crying. He knew why. She had found out about his parents. Her eyes darted from place to place, searching.

Afraid that it might be a trap, forced on her by her wicked stepfather, Silver Feather was afraid to step out into the open.

The colonel knew of his daughter's close relationship with Silver Feather and had tried to stop her from seeing him by forbidding Diana to leave the mansion. He repeatedly threatened to send Silver Feather away.

If Diana's stepfather had sent her out to look for Silver Feather, he might not be that far behind.

Then Diana spoke something, but her words were too soft for Silver Feather to hear.

He listened more intently when she spoke again. This time, he heard her clearly. She was saying that she was alone, that no one was following her, and to please, please, come to her.

Throwing caution to the wind, Silver Feather stepped out in front of her pony.

Diana's eyes widened in fright for a moment before she quickly slid from her saddle and flung herself into Silver Feather's arms.

"Oh, Silver Feather, I am so sorry," she sobbed

as she clung to him. "What are you going to do? Where are you going to go?"

He eased her from his arms. Their eyes met and held.

"Silver Feather, I have always known how evil my stepfather was, but I have no choice but to live with him," Diana said, another sob catching in her throat. "I have no one else but an aunt in New Town, who is very, very poor, and old. She has scarcely enough food to feed herself, much less me."

"I know that you must stay with him," Silver Feather said. He reached out to stroke her hair, enjoying the touch of its texture against his fingertips. "As I have no choice but never to return to Dettro Manor. If I do, I shall die."

"My stepfather is so angry over losing you," Diana whispered. "He sent many men out to look for you. I waited until they were all gone, then came myself when I knew no one would be able to follow me. Oh, Silver Feather, what are you going to do? Where are you going to go? I shall miss you so much. Silver Feather, I shall die without you," she cried, clutching him to her body. "I shall die!"

"No. You have much to live for," Silver Feather said, reveling in the feeling of her in his arms, for he knew it would be the last time. He had to get as far from this place as possible.

"But how can I?" Diana cried. "I have lived only for our moments together."

"Diana, I have no choice but to go without you," Silver Feather said, his voice almost failing as his emotions ran rampant. "I do not know where my travels will take me. I know of no other Choctaw village. All that I know is that I must avoid your stepfather at all costs, for if he finds me, he will shackle me for running away. He will beat me before . . . before . . . he kills me."

"Please do not say such things," Diana said, shuddering. "Please do not speak of . . . death. It cannot happen, Silver Feather. It cannot happen to you."

"I will not be dying anytime soon," Silver Feather reassured her. He stepped away from her, yet still held her soft hands in his. "I know the skills of survival. I will survive. Do not doubt that, Diana. Never doubt that."

"What can I do to help?" she asked, searching his eyes.

"There is one thing . . ." he said, now wondering if he dared suggest something that might in the end bring harm to her.

"Tell me. What can I do? You know that I will do anything. Anything!"

"You can go with me into the secret passageway one last time," he said, growing excited about the prospect of what they might achieve.

"Truly?" Diana gasped.

"Yes, truly," Silver Feather said, his eyes beaming as hope came into his heart.

"But why?" she asked softly. "You said only moments ago that you should not be anywhere near the plantation, much less enter the passageways of Dettro Manor."

"I heard my mother and father talking only last night about papers that might prove how your stepfather cheated my people," he said in a rush of words. "Diana, those papers are surely among your stepfather's things somewhere. If I have proof that the land of my ancestors is still theirs, I can take it to the authorities at New Town. Then finally the nightmare will be over."

"It will be dangerous for you to go to Dettro Manor," Diana warned. "Are you sure you wish to do this?"

"If you are willing to take me, I am willing to risk my life for my people," Silver Feather said, nodding.

"Well, since the passageway entrance is so far from the manor house, I believe I can successfully sneak you into it, but only after dark and after I have made certain that no one is standing guard around the grounds."

"Yes, we must be more careful than ever before," Silver Feather agreed.

"Silver Feather, I brought some food from the kitchen," Diana said, opening her saddlebag. "In case I found you."

She yanked a bundle from the saddlebag and handed it to Silver Feather. "I must take my pony into hiding. Come. We can eat and talk until it is safe to go to the passageway."

They settled down beside a small stream, where weeping willows hung long and low all around them, giving them the privacy they needed. They ate, and talked, and hugged. Then, when they thought it was close to the midnight hour, they headed back toward Dettro Manor.

"What if your stepfather missed seeing you before bedtime?" Silver Feather asked as he rode on the pony with Diana.

"I heard him give orders to his men telling them that they would ride far and wide until they found you, and that none of them should expect to sleep in a bed tonight. Then he rode out with them," Diana answered. "Silver Feather, once we arrive in the passageway, you must stay for a while. Surely in a few days, my stepfather will give up. It will give me time to search and for us to be together, for once you are gone, who is to say when we will see one another again?"

"Yes, I believe he will not give up until he thinks that I am long gone," Silver Feather said. "And all the while, I will be right beneath their noses with you."

Close enough to Dettro Manor to see the lamplight in some of the windows, they dismounted and led the pony on foot into the passageway.

They walked for some time in the dark, before

Diana stopped and grabbed Silver Feather by an arm.

"It will be safe enough to take you on into the attic," she said. "My stepfather never goes there and you will be more comfortable. But I won't be able to bring blankets and food until later. I can't do too much at once or one of my stepfather's household staff might get suspicious and tell him that I'm up to something. We'll take Mama's patchwork quilt. That should keep you warm enough."

"Thank you, Diana, for risking so much for me," Silver Feather said. "Please be careful."

"I shall begin my search for the papers tomorrow," Diana said softly. "But only after I bring you food."

"Diana, my Diana," Silver Feather said, drawing her into his embrace.

When she lifted her lips to his and kissed him, they were stunned by the result. She leaned away from him and gazed into his eyes as he gazed into hers.

They realized that they were in love, and surely had been even since those earlier days together. She had been four and he was eight when they had found each other beside a lake. He was still free and living with his people at his village.

They had formed a special bond then, swimming in the lake, nude, laughing, giggling, and learning about one another.

But now? They knew that what they shared was true love.

"I must succeed at finding those papers. I must be able to be your Goddess of the Hunt!" Diana said with tears in her eyes.

They moved into each other's arms and kissed again, shyly this time, before moving through the passageway into the manor. Diana cautiously led the way until they finally reached the attic.

Moonlight wafted through the one lone window high on the wall of the attic, as they gazed at one another. Suddenly, Diana turned and rushed from the room, leaving Silver Feather alone.

"One day you will be my wife . . . my Goddess of the Hunt," he whispered, feeling wonderfully at peace within himself, his heart filled with his Diana.

Chapter 3

Sudden, thy shadow fell on me;
I shrieked and clasped my
Hands in ecstasy!
    —Percy Bysshe Shelley

"I'm so sorry that I couldn't find the papers," Diana said as she stood with Silver Feather, the lamp in her hand flickering its soft, golden light on his sculpted face. "It's been several days now, and I'm no closer than when I started. And I can't get into my stepfather's safe. He guards the combination with his life."

"I am just glad that you did not get caught," Silver Feather said, trying to absorb these last moments with her before saying a good-bye that might be their last.

He had no idea where his travels would take him once he left Dettro Manor, or how far. Except for lovely, sweet Diana, he was alone in the world, and when he left the passageway this time he knew the chances were that he might never see her again.

He reached a gentle hand to her face and savored touching its softness. He would never forget the kiss that made them both aware of their strong feelings for one another regardless that they were children. Inside their hearts and minds they were as committed to each other as any who repeated their vows on their wedding day.

"I shall miss you so," he said, his voice breaking as it wavered between that of a young brave and that of a mighty Choctaw warrior.

Fighting to keep the courage of a man within him, he dropped his hand. Diana set the lantern on the oak floor of the attic and moved gently into his arms.

"Hold me," she whispered, clinging to him. "Please, hold me. How can we say good-bye? It . . . it . . . isn't fair."

"So much in life is not fair, Diana," Silver Feather said, gently caressing her back. "But one must live with what life offers and make the best of it."

"I hate it," Diana said, a sob lodging in her throat. "I hate what has become of your life and mine. Surely there is something we can do. . . ."

"No, nothing," Silver Feather said. He stepped away from her so that he could look into her beautiful blue eyes.

He had memorized everything about her and would carry it with him.

He had lost his beloved parents and his Eagle

Clan, and now he was losing the only girl that he would ever love.

"I must leave now," Silver Feather said, taking her hands in his, holding on to them as long as possible. "The longer I am here, the more danger there is of our being discovered."

"What will you do?" she asked, her voice trembling as she fought a strong urge to cry. "Where will you go?"

"I hope to find a Choctaw clan that has had better luck than mine," Silver Feather answered, "though perhaps I should not ask anyone to accept me. I might bring trouble to them should your stepfather's search lead him there."

"But that might mean that you will have to live alone," Diana said, her voice breaking again. "Please don't think of others first, as you are prone to do. You must find a people that will take you in."

"I am strong, Diana." Silver Feather tried to reassure her of that. "I will be able to survive anything, even this, if I am forced to."

"If only I could have found those papers," Diana said, sighing.

"I would not want you to chance looking any longer," Silver Feather said, drawing her into his embrace again, just needing the feel of her against him once more. "I must leave. Now."

She lifted the lantern, then smiled at him when he took her free hand. Nothing else was said as they worked their way through the manor and then the dark, dank passageway until they saw the moon's glow at the far end.

Diana had waited until the midnight hour to go to the attic tonight, for she knew that was the safest time for Silver Feather to make his escape.

When they reached the opening, there was a horse ready for him, saddled, and with two heavy bags of provisions hanging from each side.

"The horse will be missed," Silver Feather said, turning to her, seeing the shine of tears in her eyes. "I should not take it."

"I doubt that my stepfather will be told about its absence," Diana said, flicking a tear from her eye. "The stableboy is guilty of having stolen two horses recently. I know. I saw him taking them. But I did not report him, for it gave me an idea. Harry would not dare mention this to my stepfather, for it would draw attention to the other two being gone."

"And your stepfather does not keep any closer eye on his steeds than that?" Silver Feather asked, his eyes widening.

"He has so much more on his mind than horses," Diana said.

They embraced again. "Silver Feather, please remember that when you are old and gray, I will still be your Goddess of the Hunt. In my heart, you will always be with me."

"As you will be in mine, too," Silver Feather

said, then placed a finger beneath her chin and lifted it so that their lips could meet.

They kissed and clung together, then Silver Feather pushed himself away from her and swung into the saddle.

Holding the reins, he gave Diana a lengthy gaze, then wheeled the horse around and rode away, the midnight-black steed blending in with the night so that Diana soon lost track of him.

Sobbing so hard that her body shook, she turned and walked back inside the passageway where she allowed herself to mourn the loss of her true love before quietly making her way back to her own room. She went to a window and raised it. Her heart pounding, she peered into the moon-shrouded night. Although she knew that Silver Feather must be far away by now, she still tried to see him. She saw only the trees.

Diana sat in the window seat, enjoying the magnolias with their sweet-perfumed blossoms and the intoxicating drifts of daphne and honeysuckle that rolled in on the cool breeze. She rested her head against the window frame and allowed her heavy eyes to close.

A knock on the door startled her awake.

"Who's there?" she called, as she closed the window softly.

"Diana, it is I, your father," her stepfather said through the door. "I was on my way from the library when I saw lamplight under the bottom of your door. May I come in, Diana? I have something to say to you."

Panic filled her again.

She should be dressed for bed, not wearing this lovely silk thing with pretty flowers embroidered at the hem.

"Just a moment, please," she said. "Let me make myself decent."

She scrambled out of the dress, tossed it into her chifforobe, closed the door, and hurried into a robe.

She eyed her bed. She quickly yanked the bedspread from it and hurriedly folded it, then patted the mattress and pillows to make it look as though she had been there.

She sucked in a wild breath, then went to the door and opened it.

Her stepfather stood there, wearing his monogrammed nightshirt and the same breeches that he had had on all day. He also wore his fancy house slippers, and he held a bound book in his left hand.

"I was finding it hard to sleep," he said in an odd voice. "I went to the library for a novel."

Then he smiled what she thought was a wicked smile as he stepped into the room.

"I've received some information I thought might interest you," he said.

"What is it? Couldn't it wait until morning?" Diana replied, feeling intruded upon at this time of night, especially when the caller was a man she loathed with every fiber of her being.

"I wanted to tell you that your little friend is dead," Jamieson said, watching her flinch and take a shaky step away from him.

Diana felt as though she might faint. She grabbed the door and clung to it, lest she crumple to the floor.

She fought back the tears that were burning in her eyes, for she did not want to give this evil man the satisfaction of knowing how much he had upset her.

"Just thought you'd be able to get past missing him if you knew he was dead, for it is best, you know, to forget him," Jamieson said, smiling smugly.

"How? When . . . ?" she asked, imagining that he had been gunned down tonight without even the chance to defend himself.

"A few days ago he was found hiding not that far from my fields of cotton," Jamieson said. Diana let out a strange sort of gasp. "I, myself, shot him on the spot. Good riddance of bad rubbish, I'd say."

"A few days ago?" Diana asked in barely a whisper. She wanted to kick him and spit in his face for telling such a lie.

"Yep, and now you can go back to bed knowing that he's in the ground next to his parents,"

Jamieson said, turning and walking from the room. "Sleep tight, dear."

Diana listened to his footsteps until he entered his room and closed the door behind him, then she closed her own door and rushed to the window.

"Silver Feather," she whispered. "Please go far away from this place. I promise that we will meet again. We must, for I love you so dearly!"

Chapter 4

Come, slowly, Eden!
Lips unused to thee,
Bashful, sip thy jasmine,
As the fainting bee.
 —Emily Dickinson

The Mississippi Valley Region—1825

Years had passed since Silver Feather had said his last good-bye to Diana, yet in his heart it seemed only yesterday.

He had carried her image with him everywhere he went, knowing there was very little chance that they would ever meet again.

He rarely ventured back in the direction of Dettro Manor, even though he had left his heart there. He had always known that if her stepfather saw him, he would be killed on sight. Surely it had been an embarrassment to that powerful man that one of his Choctaw "slaves" had slipped away as easily as Silver Feather had done.

Silver Feather knew not to pursue Diana, even though the memory of her and their kisses sent warmth into his heart. But his midnight dreams were filled with her. He knew that she had grown into a woman and surely was so beautiful that she made all men's hearts melt.

Had she married? Where was she now? Did she ever think of him?

Even though Silver Feather was twenty-five winters of age now, he had not married. He had not been able to put Diana out of his heart, though he knew how futile it had been to keep thinking about her.

He had also not been able to put his need for vengeance out of his mind. However, he did not want to bring trouble to the Turtle Clan who had taken him in, so he had done nothing.

The Turtle Clan were a happy people, away from the rule of any man with white skin. They were the lucky ones, for many red men were still being tricked and were losing their land.

As Silver Feather sat in council with his Turtle Clan, he tried to concentrate on what was being said, yet he could not. After several nights of dreaming about his Eagle Clan's bone house, he was planning to return to the land that had once belonged to his Eagle Clan.

He pined to pray beside his clan's bone house, where so many of his ancestors' bones had been placed through the years. It was as though he was being beckoned there.

Enough time had passed now that no one from

Dettro Plantation would recognize him. He had probably been forgotten long ago.

Silver Feather had sent a scout to venture close to Dettro Manor to observe who came and went from it. He knew that much had changed there.

From the information the scout reported, Silver Feather doubted that either Colonel Dettro or Diana lived there now. The scout told him that the land and house were in ruins.

Praying at the bone house on the land at Dettro Manor surely would not bring trouble to the Turtle Clan. They lived in peace with whites, especially since they lived so far from any town or homestead.

The Turtle Clan was well established at their village beside a lake, surrounded on three sides by the wooded hills of Mississippi and by the lake on the fourth, except where they had their crops planted.

They existed without aid or interference from whites. They made their own clothes and had huge gardens. They had enough wood, taken from the dense forest, for firewood and homes and eating utensils.

The only thing they had from the whites was a few stolen horses, which were their mode of travel—though there was no need even to steal horses from whites any longer. The Turtle Clan now bred their own.

He owed so much to the Turtle Clan. After riding away from Dettro Manor—sometimes feeling as though he was riding in a circle—Silver Feather had come upon the hidden village deep in a forest beside a mystically beautiful lake.

He had been welcomed and, surprisingly, had discovered that the chief of the Turtle Clan was kin to him. He was a second cousin to Silver Feather's beloved father.

Silver Feather had worked his way up in the Choctaw Turtle Clan to be first a warrior of great importance and then their chief.

"Chief Silver Feather?"

A voice speaking his name brought Silver Feather out of his deep reverie.

He blinked his eyes, gazed around him, and saw his warriors sitting dutifully in a half circle around the fire in the large council house, their eyes studying him.

"Chief Silver Feather, we do not feel that it is safe for you to travel alone," White Cloud said, drawing Silver Feather's eyes to him. "We have heard you speak of your dreams and of traveling to your Eagle Clan's bone house. We understand your need to be there. But it is near the people you fled from those years ago. Is it wise to go there again?"

Silver Feather flipped his thick black hair back from his shoulders so that it fell down far past his waist, held in place by his beaded headband. A lone feather hung from a coil of hair at his left side.

He wore fringed buckskin clothing and ankle-high buckskin moccasins.

"As I have told you, it is as though I am being beckoned to my ancestors' bones," he said. "There has to be a reason why. There is only one way to know, and that is to go and see if the bone house remains untouched by whites."

"Let me accompany you," White Cloud, his best friend, said, his eyes anxious.

"That is not necessary," Silver Feather said. "It is I who had the dreams. It is I who am being beckoned, so I shall go alone."

"You know that we trust you in all things, my chief, but must we remind you again of what happened to your Eagle Clan? You might be the only survivor. If the man who claimed your parents' lives, who enslaved the rest of your clan as though they were no more than animals, believes you are in the vicinity, surely he will come after you."

"I was an elusive young brave who was able to escape his clutches," Silver Feather said. "I am now a mighty warrior—a chief. I assure you that I will be safe."

He paused, then said, "Do not concern yourselves with the possible danger of Colonel Dettro. I do not believe he is a part of the manor any longer."

He had told some of his closest friends of his relationship with Diana, and he knew that those select few believed that he was going back to try once again to see the white woman. But that wasn't true. He truly believed that she no longer lived at Dettro Manor—although he would give many horses to see her again.

"I must go now," Silver Feather said, rising. He stood over them, looking each individual in the eye. "Do not worry about your chief. Trust in my judgment."

Everyone nodded and did not rise to walk with him from the lodge.

His white steed was ready for him, waiting just outside the huge council house. It was saddled, and a buckskin bag of provisions hung on one side of the saddle.

He swung himself onto the stallion, took the reins in hand, and rode from the village. This was the son of the very horse that Diana had stolen those long years ago for his escape. That horse had taken him to freedom. Now White Lightning was taking him back to a land of heartache.

But he did need this time with his ancestors' spirits.

He *must* find out why he had seen his Choctaw Eagle Clan bone house more than once in his dreams.

Silver Feather rode the rest of the day and into the night until finally he arrived on land that had once belonged to his clan.

He rode onward a short distance, his heart

pounding with anticipation as he approached the bone house. He drew a tight rein and stopped.

The moon's glow revealed many white men removing the bones from the bone house and placing them in huge trunks, then carrying them to a wagon. He grew cold inside. They were in the process of desecration.

Enraged by what was happening, yet unable to stop it since he was only one man, he watched carefully. Some men climbed aboard the wagon while others mounted their horses. Soon all of them rode away, leaving the door of the bone house open. Surely no bones remained inside.

At first Silver Feather didn't follow. Stunned by what he had seen, he could only sit there looking at the bone house.

And then an anger filled him that he had felt only one other time in his life—the day his parents had been murdered.

His jaw tight, he followed far enough behind the wagon and the men on horseback for them to be unaware of his presence.

He drew a tight rein within the cover of the dense forest and watched as the men took the wagon to the barn on the plantation grounds of Dettro Manor.

Could Diana's stepfather be involved in this terrible desecration? Was Colonel Jamieson Dettro still living at Dettro Manor after all?

Chapter 5

Up to the wonted work! come trace
The epitaph of glory fled;
For now the Earth has changed its face,
A frown is on the Heaven's brow.
                    —Percy Bysshe Shelley

The dust flew in the wind as the stagecoach traveled down a road that was filled with ruts.

Diana snapped the reins and shouted at the six horses pulling the stagecoach, groaning as she bounced on the seat again. She could not maneuver around the holes quickly enough. But that was the last thing on her mind.

A stagecoach driver now, having found herself penniless, she had been given the commission to go to the plantation where she had once lived.

She was ordered to pick up several trunks. She had been told not to question what she would be transporting. She was paid to do it.

Dressed in denim pants and a loose-fitting red plaid cotton shirt, and with her golden hair tucked up inside the tall crown of a wide-brimmed hat of the sort usually worn only by men, she looked anything but a woman. It was important since she lived in the world of men now, doing a man's job.

She was able to get around much more easily by not revealing her femininity to those she encountered in the course of her work. As long as she kept the wide brim pulled down, which helped shadow her face, and talked in a low, false voice, she managed to stay incognito.

Even the female passengers she sometimes carried in the stagecoach had no idea that they were in the company of another woman—one who hid her feelings about how she wished that she was wealthy enough to wear beautiful clothes and travel in luxury instead of on the seat with the reins in her hands.

A short time after she had said good-bye to Silver Feather, her stepfather had been gunned down, and everything in Diana's life had changed. It was not enough that she had lost the love of her life as Silver Feather had ridden away from her, but she had lost everything else, too.

There had been no written will that she could find that could have protected her. As far as she knew, she had gotten nothing.

She had been taken in by her widowed aunt in New Town. There she had lived poorly, subsisting day to day on whatever money her aunt could earn by making bread for those in New Town who would buy it.

Diana's thoughts were stilled when she came in

sight of what had once been Dettro Manor. This was not the first time she had seen it since she was a little girl, but she was sick at heart all over again as she saw everything that once was so grand in such disrepair.

The cotton fields were overgrown. The house was in need of painting. Weeds grew up tall around the house where stately magnolia trees had once prevailed, their limbs heavy with fragrant blossoms.

It was unbelievable that the people who took residence after she left to live with her aunt had neglected everything so much.

She pushed onward in the moonlight, down the long lane that led to the house.

Now that she was back "home" again, she was swallowed up by memories—memories of her mother when she had been alive and happy even though she was married to one of the cruelest men in Mississippi. At least Colonel Jamieson Dettro had treated Diana's mother gently and lovingly.

Tears came to her eyes as she suddenly recalled those times in the hidden passageways of the manor with Silver Feather. She could almost feel his presence as she recalled those earlier days together. But Silver Feather was gone, and Diana had come to believe she would never see him again.

She had lived with that, the knife digging deeper into her heart each day as she thought of that sweet Choctaw brave, his smile so wonderful, his laughter so infectious, ripped away from her.

"Damn you to hell," Diana whispered to her stepfather as she rode closer and closer to the tall, pillared house.

Yes, because of Colonel Jamieson Dettro, many lives had been ruined—Silver Feather's, his people's . . . and her own.

Those years when she had lived with her aunt, worrying about when they would next eat, had taught Diana the art of survival.

She had made friends with others who were as poor and unfortunate as herself, who also felt the need to find a way to survive this cruel world.

She had learned how to cook almost anything and how to blend into a crowd. When she had heard about the stagecoach job, she had grabbed it and had been working ever since. When her aunt passed away from the same heart ailment that had killed Diana's mother, Diana had been on a run.

The heart condition was a killer, especially to people like her mother and aunt, whose frail bodies could not fight back and overcome it. Diana made certain that she ate the right foods and got the right amount of exercise, which she knew was required to stay healthy and strong. When she had children she would see that they did the same.

"When I marry . . ." she whispered to herself.

She got a lost, sad look in her eyes when she recalled Silver Feather's telling her that he would gather a bouquet of bluebells for her to carry on their wedding day. Diana couldn't bear to consider marrying anyone else. How could she? She had been born to love, to marry, only one man.

Luckily Diana's work as a stagecoach driver was lucrative. The only problem with her situation was the constant danger of being discovered. She had been driving a stagecoach for a year now, and thankfully, thus far no one had guessed that she was a woman.

She glanced down at her holstered pistols. They were her constant companions. She never went anywhere without them.

And she was dead accurate with the shotgun she kept concealed on the stagecoach. No one would want to go up against her.

But how she missed the feminine side of her life. She ached to wear dresses and to tie lovely satin bows in her hair again. She would just die for a bottle of the French perfume that her rich women passengers wore, the luscious smell wafting up to where she sat while driving them to their destinations.

But Diana owned no dresses, no satin ribbons, and especially no French perfume.

The only pleasures in her life now were an occasional good piece of juicy beef and fried potatoes, a soft, warm bed, and a hot bath.

As Diana started to pull up in front of what had

once been called Dettro Manor, a strong urge to cry overwhelmed her.

All of the pillars that had once stood so stately along the long, wide porch were weather-beaten and gray. The windows above the roof of the porch looked as though they were eyes gazing sadly down at Diana as lamplight glowed from within.

Her gaze fell upon the window of the room that had been hers those many years ago. She had stood there so often looking out over the cotton fields and watching horses grazing, smelling the fragrance of magnolias.

"It's all gone," she whispered, tears burning in her eyes. "How could anyone let this happen?"

The front door opened and a man she despised stepped out onto the porch, a lighted kerosene lamp in his right hand.

Chapter 6

Love and Harmony combine,
And around our souls entwine.
— William Blake

Just as Silver Feather managed to get closer to the barn without being seen by the white men, he saw the stagecoach arrive at the front of the plantation house.

He watched now as the driver got down from the seat and was greeted by a man who came from within the house.

Silver Feather maneuvered close enough to see that the man wasn't Colonel Dettro, but instead some other unsavory-looking person. As he stepped down closer to the stagecoach driver, he said something that made the driver take a step away from him.

Many feelings rushed through Silver Feather as he surveyed the plantation for the first time in eleven years. Everything was overgrown with weeds, and the house was neglected. His scout had been correct. Silver Feather doubted that

Diana's stepfather owned it any longer. Which meant Diana was gone.

Then he gazed back to where the slaves' cabins had once been. Most had collapsed in rubble to the ground.

He looked to the building where the cotton had at one time been weighed and a quick anger seized him as he recalled the day his parents had lost their lives. He had not even had the chance to see to their burial.

Now he knew why he had hesitated to return to this place of sad, tormenting memories. It was not so much a fear that Colonel Dettro might discover him and finish what he had not been able to do those long years ago, but it was more that his feelings were still raw. And Silver Feather knew that if he ever saw the colonel again he would be tempted to kill him.

He tore his eyes away from the building. It was eerily quiet. Where was the rest of his Eagle Clan? Had they been sent away or had they been methodically murdered, one by one, until there was no one left?

Noise at the barn startled him out of his thoughts. The trunks of bones were being loaded on the top of the stagecoach by the men who had stolen them from the bone house, while the driver and the man stood and watched.

After the trunks were secured on top of the stagecoach, riders on horseback left, while the driver and the unsavory man went inside the house.

Silver Feather weighed his options. He could listen at the window to what was being said, or he could try to take the stagecoach himself. He doubted he would learn anything useful from eavesdropping, nor did he have a place to hide the bones. He realized that it was best to wait until the stagecoach left the plantation grounds with its precious cargo. Then he would follow it. He must find out where the bones were being taken, and to whom. After he knew, he would gather many of his warriors and rescue them.

What the white men had done was sacrilegious. How could they have entered the sacred bone house and taken the bones of a people as good and precious as his Choctaw Eagle Clan? How could any white man step inside a house where spirits of the Choctaw's past hovered and watched?

He gazed heavenward. He listened to the wind.

In the soft breeze he thought he heard a moan of despair.

"I shall make it right for you!" he whispered, suddenly feeling something brushing against his face, as though someone had come to him and caressed him.

He gazed quickly at the house when he heard a mocking laugh. He wondered which of the two men had laughed in such a way.

Again he was tempted to go closer to the window and listen, but he knew the dangers in doing that.

He sighed, and his jaw tightened as his impatience grew. But he kept reminding himself to remain calm. If he was caught now, the bones of his people would be lost forever. He had a mission.

He had to save his clan's bones and return them to where they had been for many generations of Choctaw.

Chapter 7

Diana was standing in what was once her stepfather's office. She stood in front of Colonel Dettro's old desk, while Harry Braddock stood behind it.

She tried to fight off the feelings from her past that were assailing her. That part of her life had died long ago.

"Stop with your jokes. Let's just get this over with so I can be on my way," Diana said in her gruffest voice, being sure to keep the brim of her hat low. "I don't find you funny at all." She reached a gloved hand out toward him. "Give me the papers and the instructions as to where to take this shipment."

"You don't like me much, do you?" Harry Braddock said, taking a dangerous step closer to her as he came from behind the desk. "What's not to like about me? Ain't I pretty, young fella?"

"Just hand me the papers so I can be on my way," Diana insisted, her heart pounding.

The man who owned Dettro Manor now was the complete opposite of the man who had owned it when she was a small girl.

Colonel Jamieson Dettro had prided himself in how he dressed and how he ran his plantation.

This man with the greasy brown hair and mocking smile had let the plantation go to waste. Dettro Manor itself was shamefully ruined and smelled strangely of something she could not identify.

"Now why would a young thing like you be so uncomfortable with a man of my means?" Harry said. "This house used to be a pretty sight in its heyday, and I could make it grand once again if you'd stay and be a part of it."

"What?" Diana gasped, her eyes widening.

She flinched as Harry grabbed her hat from her head, causing her golden hair to fall to her waist.

"Gotcha," Harry said, his pale green eyes gleaming. He tossed the hat aside. "I always thought you were a woman. Your facial features are much too pretty. You guarded the secret well enough until tonight. You made a mistake coming into the house, where the light is better. You kept tugging on the brim of that hat, but it didn't help any."

He took a step closer. "Come on, give me a kiss," he said, puckering his lips in a way that disgusted Diana so much she visibly shuddered.

"Get away from me," Diana said, stepping quickly back from him. "You disgust me. I've despised you from the moment I saw how little respect you have for Dettro Manor."

"And how do you know so much about this house?" Harry asked, raising a shaggy eyebrow.

"Because I lived here," Diana said, proudly lifting her chin.

"You?" Harry asked, kneading his chin in contemplation.

"My stepfather was Colonel Jamieson Dettro," Diana said defiantly. "I lived here until he was gunned down."

"Is that so? Then why didn't you inherit the place?" Harry asked, smiling slowly. "Or should I ask? He disinherited you, didn't he?"

"That's not the way it was at all," Diana said, swallowing hard.

Realizing that she was debating with this man, a man she truly despised, she stopped talking momentarily, trying to control her emotions.

"Just give me my payment and those papers, and tell me what I'm to do with this shipment, then I'll be on my way," she said again. She eyed her hat, then grabbed it from him and tucked her hair beneath it again. "I need to leave. I'm late getting started as it is, and I don't like traveling at night."

"You wouldn't have to if you'd marry me," Harry blurted out. "I've been without a wife for some time now. Marry me and I'll restore this place for you. You'll be my queen."

"I would rather be dead than share anything with you," Diana spat out. "Now *please* let me be on my way."

"Like I said, if you'd marry me, you could live in this mansion again," he said, holding the papers behind him.

"Mansion?" Diana said, then laughed sarcastically. "It's no mansion now. It's a disgrace what you have done to it."

"I'd let you restore it to its full glory if'n you'd marry me," he insisted. "Look at you. You're wasted as a stagecoach driver. You'd make a beautiful belle of this manor. I'd give you everything."

"What sort of work do you deal in?" Diana asked suspiciously. "You have no slaves, no cotton. What's in those trunks that you're so mysterious about?"

"If you marry me you could know everything about me and my business dealings," Harry said. "You could even be my partner. Otherwise, it's none of your concern."

He paused, then said, "It's government-issued— top secret," his eyes twinkling.

Diana laughed again. "I know a liar when I see one."

Harry stepped closer and leaned his face close to hers. "You'd best mind your manners."

Diana felt the threat deep in her gut and knew

that she had said all she dared to say. Now that
Harry knew she was a woman, he could even take
advantage of her, and no one would be there to
stop him.

Diana swallowed hard. "Give me the rest of the
instructions and my money, and I'll be on my
way."

Harry went behind the desk and pulled a bag of
coins out of the safe, then slapped it into Diana's
hand.

He hurriedly told her the instructions.

"You can go now, but you might want to think
on my proposal," he said, as he walked her from
his office and on out to the porch. "I'd marry you
in a minute."

Diana gave him an amused look, then rushed
down the steps.

Harry's face grew red as he watched her climb
aboard the stagecoach and drive away. "You
witch," he whispered under his breath. "No one
treats Harry Braddock like that and gets away
with it. I'll get you the next time we come face-to-
face."

Chapter 8

Virtue, how frail it is!
Friendship, how rare!
—Percy Bysshe Shelley

Silver Feather followed the stagecoach, but stayed far enough back that he could not be seen. His eyes widened when a sudden spattering of gunfire came from the dark shadows of the trees on the side of the road.

He immediately fell farther back so that he would not get caught in the gunfire, but he stayed close enough that he could still see the stagecoach.

When several heavily armed, masked men burst from the forest and positioned themselves on each side of the stagecoach, Silver Feather realized that the stagecoach driver was being ambushed by highwaymen, the worst of robbers.

He drew a tight rein and had no choice but to watch what was happening. One man had no chance against so many highwaymen.

His gaze went to the driver of the stagecoach. The man understood that he was outnumbered, and he didn't attempt to grab his rifle to defend himself. Instead, he stopped the stagecoach.

Silver Feather watched as the driver was forced at gunpoint to climb down from the stagecoach. Silver Feather nudged his mount to the right and rode quietly amid the trees, trying to get closer to the action.

He saw the driver standing with his hands in the air as four of the masked men went atop the stagecoach and cut the straps that had secured the trunks.

One by one they opened the trunks, then looked down at the stagecoach driver, dumbfounded.

"What sort of trick is this?" one of the masked men shouted. "There ain't no money in these trunks, only old dried-up bones."

So frightened that her legs were shaking, Diana found it hard to speak. But knowing the danger that she was in, that she might be shot at any time, she finally managed to respond. She used as manly a voice as she could muster.

"Bones?" Diana said, careful to keep her hat low and glad that the darkness was helping shadow her face. She prayed silently that the moon wouldn't reappear right now.

"I'm as surprised as you are," she went on. "I am paid to transport, not to look."

"Bones!" the men said, then broke into a fit of laughter as those atop the stagecoach climbed down and mounted their steeds.

One of the other men spoke. "What sort of shipment is that? Who'd have any need of old, stinking bones?"

Laughing, they all rode off, leaving Diana alone with a shipment that truly puzzled her. But she was relieved that the men had left quietly.

She held her face in her hands as she fought back the tears. She had been so afraid that she might have been living her last moments of life.

She lifted her eyes from her hands quickly when she heard a noise behind her—a snapping of a twig and then the whinnying of a horse.

Oh, Lord, had one of the masked men dropped back to kill her?

She turned. She felt the color drain from her face as an Indian rode free of the shadows of the trees, his bow notched with an arrow. She stared at him, her heart pounding in her chest.

"What do you want of me?" Diana said in a voice that she hoped would fool the Indian into believing she was a man. She had heard about Indians taking women captive.

"Turn your back to me," Silver Feather said, planning to tie up the man and take what was his.

He eyed the holstered pistols at the driver's waist, and then looked at the man again.

"Very carefully take one pistol and then the other from your holsters and drop them to the ground," Silver Feather said. "And then put your back to me."

"And if I refuse?" Diana said stiffly. "Will you kill me?"

"I do not plan to kill you, but I cannot leave an eyewitness as to who stole your shipment from you," Silver Feather said tightly.

"But you have to know that there is nothing valuable in those trunks," Diana argued. "Surely you heard the men laugh. Why on earth would you want bones?"

"Time is wasting," Silver Feather said.

The clouds that moments ago had covered the moon were now sliding away, making the night almost as bright as day. The Indian was very close, and Diana was suddenly reminded of Silver Feather.

Surely Silver Feather would have been this handsome. He had had the same classic features that were already as noble at fourteen as this man's were now.

Slowly her hands went to one pistol and then the other. She dropped each on the ground, took one last look at the handsome Indian, then turned slowly around, her back to him. She stiffened as she waited to see what he would do with her.

She knew that if he wished, he could kill her now and not have to be bothered with taking her with him wherever he was going.

Out of the corner of her eye she saw his moccasined foot kick her pistols away from her. He grabbed her wrists and soon had them tied with a rope.

"Now I am going to help you back on the stagecoach," Silver Feather said. "I am not only taking the trunks. I am taking the stagecoach and horses as well."

He paused, then said, "Also you."

Diana's hopes died at those words. She was going to be a captive!

She hoped that her hat wouldn't fly off her head when he helped her onto the stagecoach, for she wasn't quite ready for him to know that she was a woman.

She was glad when she was finally seated on the stagecoach, her eyes watching him guardedly as he tied his horse's reins to the back of it.

Silver Feather started to climb onto the seat next to the little man, but stopped to focus on the pistols on the ground. Knowing their value, he grabbed them and placed them on a seat inside the stagecoach, then climbed aboard and sat down next to the man. He took the reins, made a sharp turn left, and drove off the road.

He made his way through the forest where there was a large clearing. His plan was to take the stagecoach to his village where his warriors would help unload the trunks, then burn the stagecoach.

They would take the bones from the trunks and transport them by travois back to his clan's bone house. He would leave sentries close by as the bones were restored to the place where they belonged. Sentries would be left there at all times to guard the house. He would give the orders to his warriors not to hesitate to kill anyone who tried to desecrate the sacred bone house again.

But what of the prisoner? he wondered to himself. He had never taken a white captive before.

In a quick decision, he decided to keep the prisoner locked up at his village for a few weeks until the thieves were taken care of. Whatever the man knew about what had transpired tonight would be taken care of by that time. Only then would it be safe to release him.

He glanced sidewise at his prisoner. He had never seen such a dainty-looking white man before, small . . . even strangely petite. He hadn't seen the prisoner's face close enough yet to assess his features. Perhaps he was young.

He shrugged. All that he cared about was making things right again for his people and their ancestors.

He believed that the driver honestly didn't know what he had been transporting tonight. He had become a victim of circumstances.

Silver Feather had planned to follow this stagecoach to its destination, to see who wanted the bones, and why.

But everything had changed when the stagecoach was ambushed and the driver was made aware of his shipment. Silver Feather did not trust him to continue with his journey.

Only then had Silver Feather thought it wise to change his plan. His main interest now was to replace the bones.

He believed, though, that in time someone would return for the bones.

And when they did, they would be sorry they had ever tampered with the holy bones of the Choctaw people. White men had already taken much from the Choctaw. They could not have the sacred bones as well.

As Diana traveled with the handsome Indian through the night, she could not help but be afraid. Was this man possibly Choctaw? She knew just how gentle a people the Choctaw were and hoped she had nothing to fear from this warrior. If he had had plans to do away with her, wouldn't he already have done it?

She glanced at him in the moonlight, again taken by how familiar he seemed to her. She wanted to ask if he had ever known a Choctaw brave called Silver Feather.

Knowing how foolish that would sound, she remained silent. She only hoped that in time he would release her.

Chapter 9

That was't that all to me, love,
For which my soul did pine.
— Edgar Allan Poe

Silver Feather and Diana were spending a chilly night among screech owls and knobby, centuries-old bald cypresses, from which Spanish moss draped in ghostly tatters. They were being serenaded by squirrel tree frogs.

Carolina jessamine vine hung from the branches of a nearby live oak, its bright yellow, funnel-shaped blossoms releasing their sweet perfume into the night air. Diana was familiar with this flower. It appeared everywhere. Scenting the air with its heady fragrance, it covered and climbed over any structure that was near it.

A campfire sent its flickering, golden light into the dark heavens. The smell of baked rabbit filled the air as Diana sat across the fire from the quiet Indian, hungrily eating the delicious meat. It had been some time since she had eaten. She had

planned to take her evening meal at Knight's Inn
on the first leg of her journey north.

She couldn't believe that her cargo had been
nothing but bones. She still didn't know why they
were so important to the Indian. She wasn't sure if
she wanted to know.

Diana wished she had had time to look over her
orders for the shipment, but Braddock had made
that impossible. Now she didn't know where those
papers were. They had probably been lost in the
encounter with the highwaymen.

She expected a fight if the people who paid for
the bones learned of their being stolen.

She gazed guardedly at the Indian, wondering
if he realized the consequences of his actions.
Didn't he know that this could bring trouble to
him and to his people?

She would never forget how Silver Feather's
Choctaw people had been treated when they had
come up against whites who knew the art of trick-
ery. So many Indians now lived on reservations because they had trusted the greedy white man.

As she pulled delicious, greasy bites of rabbit
from the bone, then chewed them ravenously, she
was careful to keep her face shadowed by the brim
of her hat. Although the moon was now hidden
behind clouds, giving Diana some reprieve, the
fire's glow was still a danger to her disguise.

She sat with her head bowed, looking up only to

take occasional glances at the handsome Indian—and he was handsome.

So much about him reminded her of Silver Feather. The sculpted features. The midnight-dark eyes. The muscles. The sleekness of his beautiful copper skin.

She recalled the first time she had touched Silver Feather's skin, mesmerized even then at her young age by its softness. It had been like touching silk, the same as he had described how touching her hair was to him.

Tears filled her eyes even now as she recalled their times together. She could not help but go back in her mind to those days when they saw no wrong in swimming nude in the lake, away from prying eyes. At that time, they had never seen each other as boy and girl. They had a relationship that went beyond being uneasy in each other's presence.

Then when they had gotten older and Diana started to blossom, they had stopped swimming altogether, bashful about their changing bodies. Instead, they rode horses when Diana could steal one for Silver Feather and he could sneak away to join her. Then that one day a stolen kiss made them aware of each other in another way. They knew then just how deep their feelings ran.

But all of that was in the past. Silver Feather was gone, possibly dead. How could a fourteen-year-old boy survive alone?

She had no idea what had happened to the rest of the Choctaw people who had been enslaved by her stepfather. She had been sent quickly away to live with her aunt and had no chance to find out.

Again she glanced over at the Indian, who seemed lost in his own deep thoughts as he ate. He had changed everything for her by abducting her and the stagecoach. She wondered what the future now held for her? Was she wrong to believe that this Indian would let her go unharmed? What would he do once he discovered that she was a woman?

Silver Feather caught the small man glancing at him occasionally over the fire, then dipping his head low, seemingly to hide his facial features in the shadows of the hat's brim.

Since he'd realized he was being taken captive, the man had rarely spoken. He seemed reconciled to what was happening.

The man seemed to display a strange sort of trust toward Silver Feather. It was as though he might have had some connection with Indians somewhere along the path of his life.

Silver Feather had even felt safe untying the man's hands long enough for him to eat. The man knew that he would not get far if he tried to escape.

Silver Feather looked at the high-topped hat and then tried to see the man's face, but without any luck. As the man ate ravenously, he kept his head low.

Silver Feather knew that it was necessary to stop for one night to rest not only himself and the stagecoach driver, but also the horses.

His own steed now feasted on tall, green grass not far from where Silver Feather had tethered him, along with the others.

Silver Feather glanced over at the stagecoach and its cargo held on top. It seemed unholy that the bones of his ancestors lay strewn and crowded in those trunks.

His jaw tightened as he looked heavenward at the dark sky.

Before, when the moon had been bright and full, he had felt comfortable with the night. But now the moon was gone and a wind had picked up speed, brisk and whining, as though the ghosts of his past were crying out in despair.

The driver started shivering as lurid flashes of lightning zigzagged in the distance. A storm threatened to bring cold rain to their campsite tonight. Silver Feather tossed the remnants of his meal into the fire, then rose to his feet and went to his parfleche, a buckskin bag, which he had placed on the ground not too far from where he had made camp for the night.

Keeping an eye on his captive to make certain he did not take advantage of the moment, Silver Feather removed two blankets from his bag.

He took them both back to where he planned to sleep. He placed one on the ground for himself, then offered the other to the man.

"This will make your night more comfortable," Silver Feather said, wishing the man would look up and let him see his eyes, for he could read a man's soul in his eyes. It would be good to know what sort of man this stranger was.

"Thank you," Diana said in the gruffest voice that she could muster.

She watched him go back to the other side of the fire, each step flexing the muscles in his legs, mesmerizing her. She could not help but stare at him and his wonderfully masculine physique. After they had made camp, he had tied her to the wheel of the stagecoach and had gone to the river and bathed. When he returned, he wore only a breechclout, which she assumed was his sleeping attire even though the air was turning chilly and damp as the storm seemed imminent.

He had not offered her the chance to bathe, and she was glad. Had she been made to undress in front of him, her true identity would have been revealed.

Although she did not feel threatened by the Indian, surely things would change were he to know that she was a woman. She would be vulnerable so far from civilization.

But it was enough to see the Indian all sleek, muscled, and clean. It gave her the opportunity to study him more closely. Still something about him seemed very familiar to her.

But she knew that it was only because of her relationship with Silver Feather those many years ago. Every time she had seen an Indian warrior since then, even in the distance, she could not help but compare him to Silver Feather.

"It is time to sleep now," Silver Feather said, going to her with a length of rope.

She flinched when he reached for one of her wrists and tied one end of the rope around it, then the other end, around one of his own. He left enough rope so that there was space between them.

"The rope will assure me that you will not try to escape during the night," Silver Feather said, stretching out on his blanket.

He leaned up on an elbow and gazed over at Diana, who sat frozen. She had not moved since he had released her from the wheel. She studied the rope on her wrist, as though she might be contemplating how she could remove it.

"Do not try to remove the rope, for I have placed it on you so that if you move too far, I shall be awakened," he said, then stretched out again on his back, his eyes watching the flashing lightning in the distance. He doubted that it was coming closer. It seemed to linger in one place.

When he turned back to the small man, still sitting, Silver Feather nodded toward the blanket. "I gave you the blanket," he said. "Use it. Rest. We rise early tomorrow to go on to my village."

He was careful not to say "Choctaw," which would identify his people. He didn't want to reveal too much to the man. It would be best if the stagecoach driver did not know the name of his tribe, especially his clan.

"I will sleep soon," Diana said in her false voice.

Silver Feather gazed up at her hat, then at Diana again. "You seem adamant about not removing your hat, but surely you will sleep better without it," he said, watching the man flinch at the suggestion. His eyebrows forked.

"I shall remove it soon," Diana said. "Please go on to sleep. I—I am too tense right now to rest."

"Tense?" Silver Feather said, his eyebrows again forking. "Do I make you afraid?"

Diana swallowed hard. How could she tell him that she wasn't afraid? How could she be when he reminded her so much of someone she had loved with every fiber of her being?

"Just please do not concern yourself about me," Diana said. "I am your captive. Isn't that enough?"

She continued to sit there, wondering just how she was going to sleep with her hat on. She couldn't remove it, not even after the Indian was asleep. What if he woke up before she did and saw her hair?

Silver Feather sighed heavily, tested the rope to see that it was secure, then glanced at the place he had left his weapons. They were set far enough away so that the little man could not get to them. He closed his eyes and fell into a sleep that included the beautiful Diana, again dreaming of her golden hair flying in the wind as she rode alongside him on her steed, as he rode White Lightning.

Diana saw how Silver Feather smiled in his sleep and wondered what he was dreaming about. But she had to take this opportunity to do more than sleep. She had yet to relieve herself.

While he slept, surely she could get far enough into the bushes to do her job. Then she would try to get the knife that she had sheathed on her right thigh beneath her denim breeches.

She made sure there was enough slack in the rope that it wouldn't jerk on his end, then crept on her knees to the bushes. Using her one free hand, she lowered her breeches, then felt the weight of the world lift from her as she did what she had needed to do for quite some time. When she was finished, she reached over and tried to unsnap the sheath to get the knife. But she couldn't do it with one hand.

And if she moved her other hand and caused it to yank on the rope, he would wake up and find her in a very compromising position—a position that would reveal her identity as a woman.

Disgruntled as she unsuccessfully tried over and over again to reach the knife, Diana finally gave up.

She pulled her breeches up in place again, then crawled back to her tempting blanket. But she didn't dare lie down. The hat would fall off.

Instead she sat beside the fire, drew the blanket around her shoulders, and fought off sleep. She didn't know how she could make it without sleep.

She nodded off for a while, her chin hanging almost to her chest, then she awakened with a start. The Indian still slept.

She gazed at him more intently. His facial features resembled Silver Feather's so much.

Suddenly he awakened and found her staring at him.

He sat up and watched her quickly lower her head so that the brim would hide her face again.

"Your name is?" he asked, his voice thick with sleep.

Diana's heart skipped several nervous beats.

"You tell me yours, then I shall tell you mine," she said, lying.

"You will give me your name. Now!" Silver Feather demanded.

Diana's heart thudded hard within her chest.

"Hunter," she blurted out. "That's all. I am called Hunter."

She had thought fast to come up with a name that would work for the moment. So much about him had caused her to think about Silver Feather and how she had always told him that she would be his Goddess of the Hunt. So Hunter seemed appropriate as a name for her.

"Hunter," Silver Feather said, nodding.

"I shall tell you my name when I feel it is safe to do so," he said, once again stretching out on his blanket, but this time unable to sleep.

He stared into the flames of the fire, unexpectedly caught up in memories of Diana, his Goddess of the Hunt.

Chapter 10

Who ever loved that
Loved not at first sight?
—Christopher Marlowe

When they arrived at the Indian village, Diana marveled at the beautiful lake close by. It momentarily took her attention away from the village that sat not far from it.

There were egrets and green herons gliding through moss-draped bald cypresses, which were set off against a carpet of green duckweed. American Painted Lady butterflies were skimming wild violets, as a whooping crane passed low overhead, its huge wings beating. Water lilies, in soft pastel colors, sent off a lovely fragrance, perfuming the air with a wondrous scent.

All in all, the lake seemed full of magic.

Then she turned her full attention to the village. It was vastly different from what she had envisioned. She had never seen where Silver Feather had lived before his people were forced to live at Dettro Plantation.

It was surrounded on three sides by a forest, yet land had been cleared for a huge garden, which stretched out away from the village.

She recognized rows of corn and green bean plants that were vining their way around poles. Colorful squash and green peppers were even now being collected from the garden by women and children as crows circled overhead, restlessly waiting for the people to be gone so that they could invade the corn crop.

There were no tepees, only cabins that were neat and clean, sitting back from the lake in a sort of disordered fashion.

As they rode farther into the village on the stagecoach, Diana saw a few young girls. Their faces were glowing like bright red autumn leaves, and their glossy braids fell over each ear as they stood with their mothers around a huge outdoor fire in the center of the village. Several large black kettles were suspended over the fire.

Other children had been running and playing, but now they stood and gaped openly at the warrior who brought the monstrous vehicle into their village, and then they looked at Diana.

She saw how adults who had been sitting and chatting at various places had stood up to stare at the approaching stagecoach.

Feeling uneasy with so many eyes on her, Diana held her head low so that her hat brim still hid most of her face in its shadow, yet not low enough for her to miss seeing a huge slab of meat cooking on another open fire. The spit turned slowly, dripping the tantalizing juices of the meat into the open flames. She surmised it was deer meat.

She could also smell corn cooking. The scent seemed to come from one of the huge black pots that hung over the fire.

As she recalled, corn had been the staple food of the Choctaw even when they lived on the plantation. They were allowed to grow their own small plots of corn between the slave cabins.

She had eaten with Silver Feather whenever she could sneak out. His mother had been a wonderful, caring, sweet woman who treated Diana as one of her own.

Her thoughts were brought back to the present when several warriors ran up to the stagecoach.

"Chief, why have you brought the stagecoach to our village?" one of the warriors asked as Silver Feather stopped the team of horses. "And who is this with you? What does this mean?"

Silver Feather climbed down from the stagecoach. "I will explain everything, but first we must get the stagecoach driver locked up," he said stiffly. "Then we will go into council to discuss things."

He nodded to two warriors. "Take the captive to the cabin that is not in use," he instructed them, nodding at a structure that sat not far from where he had stopped the stagecoach. "Nail wood over the windows and lock the driver in, then come to the council house."

"Please just let me go," Diana pleaded, making certain that her voice was still lower than what it usually was. "I am no threat to you. Please do not treat me as a captive."

Silver Feather turned to her. "For now you *are* my captive," he said tightly, "so you must be treated like one. You will be locked away from the rest of our people. When I make further plans for you, then you shall know what they are."

When the warriors came on each side of her, one of them taking her gently by an elbow as he ushered her away, Diana kept her head lower than before. Her heart was thundering inside her. In a matter of moments she might be forced to remove her hat. Then they would all know that she was a woman.

"As soon as you get the captive inside the cabin and the windows are secured, remove the ropes at his wrists," Silver Feather said. "But first take him into the forest so that he can relieve himself before he is locked away."

The blood rushed from Diana's face, and panic seized her.

"It will be done," one of the warriors said over his shoulder to Silver Feather, and they led the captive toward the dark shadows of the forest.

Diana's pulse raced. Her throat was dry.

After they were far enough from the village so

that no one could see them, the warriors stopped, and as Diana stood frozen, they untied her wrists.

"Go," one warrior said. "We will wait."

The other one grabbed her by a wrist. "But do not try to escape."

"Don't worry," Diana said in as gruff a voice as she could manage. "I understand."

They turned and walked a few feet from her and stood with their backs to her as Diana hurried behind a thick stand of bushes and finally had a moment alone. After she had finished with her business, she had no choice but to go back to the warriors.

They took her on to the cabin. She cringed as she watched them bring boards in and nail them over the two windows. Then they left her in darkness.

Trembling from fear and the slight chill, Diana stood in the middle of the floor hugging herself. She flinched as the door opened again and a warrior came inside carrying wood for the fireplace. She was relieved that they actually cared enough to make certain she would be warm.

Their concern brought back memories of Silver Feather and his Choctaw people and how kind they always were to her.

She wanted to ask whose tribe these Indians belonged to, but knew it was best not to talk unless absolutely necessary. Every time she opened her mouth she took a chance on the Indians' discovering her secret.

After the fire was built, the warrior left. Diana was a true captive now, locked up, alone. But at least she had the comfort of the fire. These nights could be cool.

She suddenly felt horribly alone. She missed her mother. She missed Silver Feather and their time together. They had enjoyed each other's company so much. But that had been too short-lived.

She looked quickly toward the door when it opened again. She made certain the hat was still secure as another warrior came into the cabin, this one carrying a nice-sized platter of food. He did not even look at Diana. He just set the food on the floor, turned around, and left, again locking her in.

Her predicament didn't seem real.

"I can't think about it," she whispered to herself, her eyes on the food. She recognized corn fritters, which Silver Feather's mother had sometimes made for their outings.

There was also a good pile of steaming corn that had been cooked, then scraped from the cob, and a large portion of meat. There were other colorful cooked vegetables, including her favorite, green beans, which she could tell had been cooked with wild onions. The smell was so tantalizing, her mouth actually watered.

Starved, Diana grabbed the wooden platter and quickly ate everything. When she was finished, her stomach was pleasantly full. Sighing, she set the empty platter on the floor and scooted closer to the fire.

She reached for her hat, then glanced at the door and shrugged. Thus far she had had enough warning when someone came to the cabin, for she could hear the door latch being slid aside. So she felt that it was safe enough to let her hair fall free, at least for a while.

She was tired of the hat. She was tired of the terrible breeches and shirt and the ankle-high shoes. She suddenly ached to be able to live the life of a woman.

And she knew why.

She was enamored of the handsome chief. She wanted to see what his reaction would be if he knew she was female—whether or not he would think she was beautiful, or alluring.

She became overwhelmed by memories of Silver Feather and started to feel guilty. Never before had she had such thoughts about another man—thoughts she knew she shouldn't have.

Chapter 11

"My warriors, everything has changed," Silver Feather said, drawing their undivided attention to him as they sat in their council house, which was a huge cabin at the far edge of their village.

A fire glowed in a large stone fireplace at one end of the room, casting light on the warriors who faced their chief.

"I had no choice but to intervene with the stagecoach and to bring the driver here amid our people. I saw no other way to keep him silent than to kill him. Being a man of peace, I could not kill to silence. Once all wrongs that occurred are corrected, I will release the man."

"I do not understand any of this," White Cloud said, standing and facing Silver Feather. "Why would you bring not only the stagecoach but also the driver? What was the stagecoach transporting that was of any importance to our Choctaw clan?"

"My Eagle Clan's ancestors' sacred bones," Silver Feather said, drawing gasps from all in the council.

"What?" White Cloud said, slowly sitting down among his brothers. "Why are they not at the sacred bone house of your clan?"

"I will explain as much as I know," Silver Feather said. "One thing I do not yet know is why the bones were stolen. My first plan was to follow the stagecoach and see where the stolen bones were delivered, but there was an ambush that changed my mind."

"Ambush?" Four Leaves asked, his eyebrows forking.

Silver Feather went on to tell them everything that had happened from the time he had arrived at his clan's bone house until he overtook the stagecoach driver, and why. "In time the man who now owns Dettro Manor will realize what has happened, but by then the bones of my clan will be back where they belong, and guarded," Silver Feather said tightly. "Then pity anyone who comes again to take them."

"But what are you going to do now?" White Cloud persisted.

"We must take the bones from the trunks, place them in a careful wrap of buckskin, then take them by travois back to their rightful resting place," Silver Feather answered.

"And the one you hold captive?" White Cloud asked. "What about him?"

"When all is well with the sacred bones, then we will set him free," Silver Feather said.

"But he can bring trouble back to our people," White Cloud said.

"We will make it clear to him that such an idea would not be wise," Silver Feather said with meaning.

The silent group nodded in understanding.

Chapter 12

A woman's face,
With Nature's own hand painted,
Hast thou, the master-mistress,
Of my passion.
        —William Shakespeare

Diana's ears perked up when she heard numerous horses leaving the village. Since so many warriors were leaving at once, she couldn't help but think this might be her chance to try to escape. The windows were boarded up, and the Indians surely wouldn't expect her to have a means of removing the boards.

"But I do," she whispered to herself, smiling as she hurried to her feet.

She shook her long, wavy hair down her back as she shoved her breeches down to her knees, then removed the knife from the sheath strapped on her right thigh.

She had worn the knife, along with her holstered pistols, for protection since the first day she took on the duties of being a stagecoach driver.

She pulled her breeches back up in place, secured them at the waist, then rushed to a window that had no pane of glass in it.

Sliding the tip of the knife into the slats of the boards, she struggled and pried until she managed to loosen one nail. Confident that her plan was working, she continued until all the nails on all the boards had been loosened. She laid her knife aside, yanked on one board, and then another. Freedom was only moments away.

"I can do it," she told herself, trying to get the courage to climb through the window. Then she hoped to steal a horse without being caught. "I can do it."

Grabbing her knife as her only weapon, she climbed through the window, then stopped with her back against the outer wall of the cabin. Breathing hard, and truly afraid of being caught, she stood there for a moment as her eyes assessed the situation.

She looked quickly to one side and saw no one there to guard her. She looked to her other side. Still she saw no one.

Her gaze moved to the dark shadows of the live oak forest, where lacy plumes of moss hung from the tree limbs like phantoms in the night. The moon was momentarily hidden behind the clouds, giving her the opportunity to make it to the cover of the trees.

Then she would circle around to the horse corral and do her best to steal a mount without being caught. She had far to go after she escaped. She needed to get to New Town, so it was imperative to have a horse.

But being on land unfamiliar to her, and having been disoriented by the route that the Indian had taken to the village, she was not certain which way even led to New Town.

She would have to take her chances and hope that her guess would be accurate.

And once she arrived at New Town, what would she do? She wasn't sure.

A part of her remembered the plight of Silver Feather's clan of Choctaw. She realized that these Indians who had interfered with her job surely had reason to do so. She just wasn't sure yet why.

The bones. It all had to do with the bones.

Yet she knew that those who owned the stage-coach would be out for blood—hers—if she didn't arrive with it intact. And Harry Braddock wouldn't be too happy when she didn't arrive at her destination with those dreadful bones.

Diana couldn't think about it now. First, she must succeed at escaping. Then she would figure out the next step.

Holding her breath, her eyes wild and wide, she broke into a mad run toward the cover of the trees. If someone discovered her, she was doomed.

Trembling with fear, she hurried between the trees until she came to a place where she could see the horses in their corral.

She hated stealing from the Indians, for she could not help but think of how so much had been stolen from Silver Feather and his people. But this was different. These Indians had wrongly taken her liberty away from her. She had a right to escape back to a free world.

She had to go through the thick, green stalks of the cornfield in order to get to the horses. Should anyone see the stalks of corn moving as she rushed through them, or hear the rustling of their leaves, she knew her plan would be quickly foiled.

She raised her eyes heavenward. "Please let me get a horse and get away from here," she prayed softly. "Please?"

She went on until she came to the outer perimeter of the horse corral. When one of the animals sensed her presence and neighed, a cold draft seemed to rush through Diana.

She stopped and peered ahead, and then from side to side. She sighed with relief when she didn't see anyone coming toward the corral.

Her knees weak, her heart pounding, she slid beneath the fence made of poles that surrounded the herd of beautiful horses. Once she was back on her feet, she approached the horse that was the closest to her. She saw that it was still saddled and wondered if someone would be coming for it soon.

Fearing that they might appear at any moment, she grabbed the reins and hurried the steed from the corral, on foot, then led him past the cornfield until she got to the blackness of the forest again.

She continued walking, leading the muscled brown stallion until she came to a clearing that ran along one side of the lake. "This is good enough," she whispered and hurriedly swung herself into the saddle.

She slid her knife into the saddlebag that hung from the one side, then patted the horse's thick neck.

"Come on, boy," Diana whispered. "Take me to freedom."

She sank her heels into the horse's flanks and rode away from the lake and into the dark, flat stretch of land that was flanked on each side by a thick forest of live oaks.

She rode on and on, knowing that to stop would be to chance being caught. She had no idea where the Indians had gone when they had left the village or what route they had taken. Should they come upon her in the night and see that she had managed to escape, what would they do with her?

She thought she'd heard one of them say they would kill her should she try.

Now that she had actually managed to escape, would they keep that terrible promise if they caught her?

Chapter 13

Mankind is composed of two sorts of men—
Those who love and create it—
And those who hate and destroy.
                                    —Jose Marti

Having ridden steadily since leaving his village, the many travois of bones still intact, Silver Feather was weary. Except for those short hours when he had slept with a captive tied to his wrist, he had not taken any time for himself since this mission started.

He knew that he could have gone about this in several different ways, but any other way would have delayed returning the bones to their true final resting place.

The fact that someone had so heartlessly desecrated his Eagle Clan's sacred bone house still seemed unbelievable to him. But he had learned long ago that white people did many things that were heinously wrong, so terribly strange, to the red man.

He hated to think that the white people might continue doing these things until they had killed off every red man in America, but he doubted that it would ever end.

Little by little, bits of land and pride were being stripped from the Indians by the United States government. The humiliation of it was so keen to Silver Feather's people, to all tribes, that Silver Feather knew he had to do this one thing. He would see to it that his people's bones were taken back to where they belonged—or he would die trying.

Silver Feather gazed heavenward. He was very aware that night was almost day again, and riding with several travois attached to horses could draw attention to the Turtle Clan of Choctaw. If a lone white man, or several, chose to stop Silver Feather and his warriors to inspect the cargo, he did not want to think about what they might do.

Perhaps they would laugh, as those who had ambushed the stagecoach did after seeing what was in the trunks. To them the bones were useless trash.

And at that moment, Silver Feather was glad that they had reacted with scorn. Had they taken an interest in them, for whatever reason, who could say what they would have done?

Suddenly, Silver Feather was aware of the scent of smoke in the air. He could see spirals of black smoke rising in slow swirls, more obvious now since daylight was lightening the sky. He rode onward as the smell increased.

White Cloud came up to Silver Feather's side on his black steed. "Should we stop and send someone ahead to see what is on fire?" he asked, deep concern in his midnight-dark eyes. "Where there is fire, there could be a white man burning something. It would not be good for any white man to see what we carry behind us on the travois."

"You are right," Silver Feather said, nodding. He gazed heavenward again, then looked at the travois.

He turned back to White Cloud. "You ride on ahead, alone," he instructed. "See what is burning. See how many white men there are. Then I will decide whether to wait until later to proceed or to go forward now and deal with those who might be a threat to us and our blessed mission."

White Cloud nodded, then sank his moccasined heels into the flanks of his horse and rode off at a hard gallop.

Blue Moon came up next to Silver Feather. "Do you wish me to go, too?"

Silver Feather shook his head in mild irritation.

"Where there is fire, when there is not a Choctaw village with its everyday large outdoor fire, there might be white men, and where there are white men, there is always trouble," said Blue Moon.

"Yes, I know that. But White Cloud will be quick. We are not that far now from the sacred bone house," Silver Feather said, his voice drawn.

"We have only a bend in the land to go, beyond those trees, and we will arrive there. We could soon have returned the bones to their rightful resting place, but now we are forced to delay what is so important to us all."

"But the deed will be done soon, and we can return to our village and our loved ones," Blue Moon reassured him.

Then Blue Moon went on, asking, "Once we are back home, what is your plan for the captive? If you release him, he might retaliate."

"We should hold him for some time, but treat him well so that when he does leave he will have no reason to hate us and bring the authorities back to us for questioning and possible arrest. What I did is a crime. Sometimes white highwaymen are hanged for it. I took a chance, that is true, but I did so for the sake of our ancestors and their bones. I had no choice."

Blue Moon nodded. "After the man is among our people for a while and sees that we are not evil, why would he still want to bring harm to us?"

"All that I know is that we must do what we must, and we will hope and pray to the Great Spirit for guidance and safety for us all," Silver Feather said. "All those years ago, when I was just a mere brave who was made to work the cotton fields alongside my mother and father, I learned that you cannot trust any white people."

He lowered his gaze when a vision of Diana

came into his mind's eye. "I was wrong to say that," he said, looking at Blue Moon. "There was a white person that could be trusted—one who was good through and through."

"Diana," Blue Moon said. He knew her name, for he was one of the trusted warriors who had known of Silver Feather's relationship with her those many years ago.

"Yes, my Diana," Silver Feather said. He gazed far into the distance, where he knew Dettro Manor now stood so mistreated, and got lost in thoughts of Diana.

Everything about her was made of sincere goodness. When she laughed, it had such sweet joy in it, like birdsongs in the trees on the first days of spring. When she had ridden beside him, her golden hair flying in the wind, he had felt as though they were the only two people in the world.

He would cherish those memories forever; in fact, it was those very memories that kept him from marriage. When he thought of taking a wife, he could not help but recall how he and Diana had spoken of marriage and how he had promised her a bouquet of bluebells on their wedding day.

All of those memories brought such pain to his heart now, for he could never fulfill that promise to his Diana. And yet Silver Feather knew he must choose a maid and marry someday. It was neces-sary. The more children that were born into the world of the Choctaw, the more possibilities there would be of sustaining the Choctaw into the future.

And he could not deny to himself that he ached to have a son that he could guide and teach—who would one day follow him into chieftainship.

His thoughts were disturbed when he saw White Cloud riding hard toward him, concern etched on his face.

Silver Feather saw the tightness with which his friend held his jaw, which meant that he was angry about something . . . or possibly hurt.

Silver Feather kneed his stallion and rode to meet White Cloud. When they came side by side, they both drew tight reins and stared intently into each other's eyes. When White Cloud didn't speak right away, Silver Feather knew that the news he had brought to his chief was not good.

Understanding hit Silver Feather like a cold splash of water thrown in his face. He looked in jerks heavenward at the smoke that was quickly filling the sky like black clouds billowing before a storm.

His heart thudded inside his chest. Surely whites had not burned the bone house as retaliation for Silver Feather having taken the bones back in his possession.

No one knew yet if the bones had been stolen or if the stagecoach had had trouble along the way and had been delayed. There would be no reason to point an accusing finger at the Choctaw if there was no evidence.

"They have set fire to your clan's bone house," White Cloud stated. "Just as I arrived at the edge of the forest, the whole building went up in flames. There is no way to save it."

"How can they be this cruel and heartless, to burn something sacred?" Silver Feather said, stunned at the news.

"It is not sacred to them," White Cloud said dryly. "Chief, I urge you to turn back. We must return to our village with the bones before the white men who set the house aflame see that we are near. If they catch us with the bones—"

"You are right," Silver Feather said, weariness weighing heavily on his shoulders.

He wheeled his horse around and gazed at his warriors, who were obediently waiting for direction. He spoke quietly in case his voice would carry.

He gave a hand signal to the warriors, then went to a small group of men to explain what had happened.

The sorrow blended with the anger in their faces, telling Silver Feather that they felt the same remorse and hate as he.

"Let us return home for now," Silver Feather said, his voice drawn. "I know now what must be done. I should have done it first and chanced delivering the bones to their sacred house, second."

"Vengeance?" White Cloud said, his eyes darkening.

"In time, yes," Silver Feather said, nodding. "But there are others that I am more interested in finding."

"Who?" another warrior asked.

"The people who are waiting for the arrival of the stagecoach," Silver Feather said. "The shipment was merely delayed, but it will finally arrive, intact."

"How can we achieve this?" White Cloud asked.

"We will return to our village and replace the trunks atop the stagecoach," Silver Feather explained. "The stagecoach will have its full run after all. At the other end of the journey there are those who are waiting for the bones. We will find the guilty party."

"But is it not too late?" Blue Moon asked, raising an eyebrow. "The stagecoach driver is locked up. He is our captive."

"We will release him from captivity," Silver Feather said, "and explain that he will need to continue his journey. In the end, he will be paid well for his services."

"We are poor people," Blue Moon said humbly. "How can we pay the driver what he will demand for his silence?"

"Yes, our people are poor in some ways, but in others, we are richer than the white people," Silver

Feather said, pride in his voice. "We have skills at gathering rich pelts in a short amount of time that we can sell at any trading post."

"And what if the driver refuses?" Blue Moon asked.

"Do not dwell on the negatives," Silver Feather said. "We will head back to the village now. We will place rocks in the trunks, so we do not chance losing the bones again. By the time the whites realize what has happened, they will be Choctaw captives!"

"Where can we safely hide the bones until another bone house is built?" Blue Moon asked.

"They can be stored in the cabin where the captive is now being held," Silver Feather said. "They will be guarded day and night until a new house is built on the sacred ground of the destroyed bone house. And we shall sweep up the ashes of the burned house and store them in the newly built house, for they deserve honor, too."

Another warrior, one who had stayed quiet until now, moved up closer to Silver Feather on his powerful steed. "To do what you suggest might bring disaster to all of our clan," Four Leaves said.

"We must take the chance in order to get to the bottom of this and stop the evil these men have done against our ancestors, once and for all," Silver Feather said.

He watched as Four Leaves edged his horse

back. He looked around his circle of men and into the depths of their eyes for their true feelings.

"From what I see in your eyes, you all feel the same as I," Silver Feather said, squaring his muscled shoulders. He gazed at the sun, which had climbed higher in the sky, then at his men again. "We must forgo food and rest in order to reach the village quickly. The stagecoach has already been delayed long enough."

He singled out those who had the travois attached to the backs of their horses. "You cannot ride very quickly. Those of us without travois must ride ahead of you. We must get back to where the stagecoach was hidden, take it out, and get it hurriedly back on the journey it was initially on. But beware of anyone who might come upon you and question you about what you are transporting. Be careful."

The warriors nodded.

Then Silver Feather and those without travois rode away at a hard gallop. Silver Feather knew that his plan was not as solid as he wished it could be. There could be many obstacles in the way—including the driver.

The driver was the key to a successful mission.

Chapter 14

On his tongue they pour sweet dew,
And from his mouth flow gentle words.
— Hesiod

Silver Feather persistently moved homeward. His steely determination kept him and his warriors sitting tall and straight in their saddles, although they were tired from the grueling ride.

He had told his warriors not to expect much rest until the mystery of the bones had been solved—and until a new bone house had been built.

Silver Feather was determined to do what was expected of him. He would not let down either his Eagle Clan, or the Turtle Clan.

He was so glad that his new clan of Choctaw understood his driving need to make things right for the clan he had been born into.

The Turtle Clan's bone house was close to their village, guarded and untouched by white men.

After the new bone house of his Eagle Clan was built, never again would white men have a chance to desecrate it.

Silver Feather's thoughts were interrupted when he saw someone approaching on horseback in the distance. It was a lone horseman, yet who was to say that more could not be somewhere close?

He feared any altercation with white people at this time, with the bones on the travois not that far behind.

Silver Feather drew a tight rein as he raised a hand in a silent command to his warriors to stop.

"A rider is approaching," he said to them. "I see only one, but there may be some behind him that are not yet in sight. We must protect the sacred bones at all costs! Go. Tell the others who have the bones in their possession to stop and hide them. They must protect the bones should an altercation occur."

A few warriors wheeled their horses around and rode off at a hard gallop to find those who were transporting the bones. Others rode up to flank Silver Feather. He had not ordered them into hiding, nor had he gone himself. He had no doubt that the rider had caught sight of them, because he had slowed his pace and seemed uncertain of what to do next.

From this distance, Silver Feather could not see much about the rider.

But when the rider suddenly turned his horse around and started back in the direction whence he had come, Silver Feather saw the color of the hair. His heart almost stopped dead inside his chest. He saw the full length of golden hair and was catapulted back in time.

He would never forget Diana's hair and how it flew in the wind when they went horseback riding together. Oh, how he had enjoyed running his fingers through her tresses. Her hair felt like silk against his skin.

He had dreamed of her so often, and in his dreams she was no longer a child, but instead a woman with the beautiful features she had been gifted with as a child.

His heart beat wildly as he kept his eyes on the retreating figure.

Something deep within him caused him to quickly nudge his horse's flanks with the heels of his moccasined feet, breaking away from the others. Although he didn't look over his shoulder at them, he knew they were stunned by his behavior. But at this moment, all that he could think about was Diana.

Surely it was a woman dressed in man's clothing, perhaps to disguise herself.

He gained quickly on the rider who seemed desperate to get away. She looked over her shoulder at Silver Feather. Yes, *her*. He now was certain that this was not a man but instead a lovely, golden-haired woman. His heart skipped several beats.

As he closed the gap, he saw more about her

that made him think that after all of these years of wondering about Diana, he just might have found her.

When he came up next to her, his eyes widened in surprise as he recognized the clothes. They were the same shirt and breeches the captive had worn.

But this time there was no hat hiding her hair, or shading her face.

Then he recognized something else.

The horse that she was riding was his. It was one of his best steeds, bred by him.

She turned her face so that he saw her profile. As he stared at her, he could not help but believe that this was Diana.

But how? Why? She had been wealthy. Now she must be poor to have to work for the stagecoach line dressed as a man.

Intrigued and determined to stop the woman, Silver Feather nudged his horse with his knees and rode quickly onward until he passed her; then he wheeled his horse in front of hers so that she was forced to stop.

They were eye to eye now. They stared at one another.

Silver Feather's heart pounded like thunder as he eased his horse back an inch or two, then rode up exactly next to the woman. He noticed how she watched him, scarcely breathing.

Silver Feather lifted his fingers to her hair and

touched it, then looked directly into her eyes
again.

"Diana?" he said, his voice quivering with emotion. "Diana, can this be you?" The words rushed
out before he gave her a chance to respond. "Is this
truly you—my Goddess of the Hunt?"

Diana almost fainted. Only one person had ever
called her Goddess of the Hunt.

She gazed into his eyes, and then slowly at the
rest of his body. As before, she saw features that resembled Silver Feather's as a child. His midnight-
dark eyes. The noble features, all grown up now
and handsomely beautiful.

"Silver . . . Feather?" she said, her eyes and
heart now filled with him.

The way she said his name made Silver Feather
know without a doubt that destiny had brought
them together again.

"Yes, I am Silver Feather," he said, consumed by
emotion. "I am that little boy grown up, yet I have
the same heart—one that has always beat only for
you and always shall."

Diana began crying as Silver Feather reached
over and took her from the horse onto his lap.
They clung together, then looked at each other.

"I thought I would never see you again," she
said, a sob lodging in her throat. "I thought you
were dead."

"Diana, I *was* dead, until now, until holding you
in my arms," he said thickly, his eyes devouring

her. "But I did not know it. I have gone through each day, mechanically, caring for my people, keeping them safe. But without you I have been nothing!"

"Silver Feather," she murmured, reaching a hand to his face, feeling the same softness of his copper skin that she had felt as a child. "Silver Feather, I have never been without you. I dream of you almost every night. My dreams have kept us together."

"And what happened to your stepfather?" Silver Feather asked.

"He died. His death changed everything in my life," Diana answered, her voice breaking with emotion. "I discovered that he left me nothing. I—I lived with a poor aunt until she passed away. I've had to work hard to survive."

She eased her hand from his face and hung her head. "Silver Feather, I am no longer that sweet and innocent little girl that you once knew," she whispered. "I—I have hardened."

He placed a finger beneath her chin and raised it so that their eyes could meet and hold. "By hardened, do you mean that you have been with . . . many men?" he asked guardedly.

Diana smiled into his eyes. "No, my love," she said softly. "By hardened, I mean that I have had to learn to be like a man to survive in a man's world. I wear men's clothing. I do a man's job."

"But yet you still have your beautiful hair," he

said, running his fingers slowly through the golden tresses again. "It is still as soft as I remembered it to be."

"I could never part with my hair," Diana said. "I always remembered how much you loved it."

"I still do, just as I have always loved you," Silver Feather said. "Ours was a special relationship, Diana. It was a friendship that turned to love long before we ever parted."

She ducked her head again. "Yes, I know." She raised her eyes to his. "And now?"

"I still love you. I want to give you your life back to live the way it was meant to be lived," he said. "Will you let me? Will you stay with me?"

"Yes, yes!" she cried. She flung her arms around his neck. "I want nothing more than to be with you! It is a miracle that we were able to find one another."

He held her for a moment longer, then leaned her away from him. "But, Diana, can you do one thing for me before discarding those men's clothes?" he asked, searching her eyes. "Or am I wrong to ask this of you? Can you help me? There is danger in what I will ask of you."

"I have faced danger head-on many times since the day I was left to fend for myself," she said. "Yes, let me help you."

She took his hand in hers. "Tell me," she said softly. "What do you want me to do? I will do anything for you. Anything."

"I would like for you to drive the stagecoach one last time," Silver Feather answered.

He explained about the bones and how they had been stolen. He told her about how he had come to live with another clan and about all else that had happened since they had last been together.

He then explained to her his plan for the bones.

"Rocks will be exchanged for the bones in the trunks?" she asked, trying to understand the plan. "You want to use the decoy to catch the men at both ends of the stagecoach run who are involved in the theft of the bones."

"Yes, and I especially want to know why they stole the bones in the first place," Silver Feather said, heaving a sigh.

"I am ready to help you," Diana said. "I will do anything I can, Silver Feather. Let's do it now. Then . . . I want time alone with you, so that we can truly talk."

"Yes. We need to talk," he said, his voice again filled with emotion.

Then he turned and gazed at his warriors, who had arrived behind him and now dutifully awaited him in silence.

He smiled at Diana. "Come. I want to introduce you to my warriors," he said. "A few of them already know of you, for I have talked about you around the night fires when we have exchanged stories of our past. You were of my past, Diana. Now you are my present and my future."

"Yes, our future," Diana said, still unable to believe that they were together.

Silver Feather lifted Diana onto the steed that she had stolen from his corral, and they went together back to the others.

After the warriors learned who she was and overcame the shock that they had imprisoned Silver Feather's lost love, they all rode again toward their village.

Diana sidled her steed close to Silver Feather's and smiled over at him. "Silver Feather, I thought you were a handsome young brave, but now, you are a more handsome man." She smiled sweetly.

"What a beautiful woman you have become," he said to her.

Then his eyes raked over her, in them a quiet amusement. "But we must do something about what you are wearing," he said, chuckling.

"After we achieve victory against those who have wronged your people, I shall want nothing more than to discard these clothes forever," she replied.

"You will wear the best doeskin, my woman," Silver Feather said.

"Your woman . . . ," Diana murmured.

"My Goddess of the Hunt," Silver Feather said, bringing her eyes back to his.

"Yes, your Goddess of the Hunt," she said softly.

Both smiling, and filled with so many emotions, they rode onward, the world having suddenly turned beautiful for the moment.

"It is wonderful to be riding with you again," Diana said, flinging her golden hair back as she gazed at Silver Feather. "I have dreamed of this moment so many times. And now it is real!"

Silver Feather smiled happily in response.

Chapter 15

So, one day more I deified,
Who knows but the world may end tonight.
                        —Robert Browning

The sun was sinking in the sky as the stagecoach rumbled along the dirt road. The inn that Diana was supposed to have arrived at the day before had just come in sight.

She drew a tight rein, stopping the team of horses, then looked over her shoulder at the Choctaw warriors.

They were riding into the shadows of the forest, where they would stay until the stagecoach left early tomorrow for its next destination. Then they would follow it along with Silver Feather.

She gazed at Silver Feather, who had ridden beside the stagecoach but now would join his warriors in hiding. Diana gave him a wavering, uneasy look. It was obvious that she was afraid about what lay ahead of her. She would be heavily questioned about her delayed arrival.

Diana hoped that the lie they had rehearsed

would be answer enough, for her life, as well as those of the Turtle Clan of Choctaw, hung in the balance.

Should the white people discover the Choctaw's role in what was happening, Silver Feather and his warriors knew to expect retaliation.

With Diana at his side, Silver Feather had had a short meeting in the council house at his village. Everyone had agreed with his plan.

"I can't help but be afraid," Diana blurted out now. "What if they don't believe me?"

"Never forget that I will be close," Silver Feather said. He took her hand as she reached for him. "I will be watching. I will be able to tell by their reaction to your arrival whether it is good or bad. If it is bad, I will immediately come for you."

"But if I fail in my part of the plan, so shall you," Diana said.

"The important thing is to make certain you are out of danger," Silver Feather said tightly. "But for now, my Diana, let us not dwell on the negative. I believe we will succeed."

He swallowed hard. "All you have to do is ask and we can turn around and return to my village. We can just concentrate on building the new bone house and on planning our marriage ceremony. For we will be married, Diana. Soon."

"When I was a mere girl in love with a young brave, I dreamed of becoming your wife, and then everything in our lives changed for the worse. My hope was gone," she said, tears shining in her eyes. "And now? We have a second chance. We can fulfill our destiny."

"Again, I say to you, if you do not want to go ahead with our plan today, we can abandon the stagecoach with its trunks of rocks and return to my village," Silver Feather said, his eyes searching hers in the fading light as the sun swept lower and lower behind the distant hills.

"I want to do what I can to make things right for you and your people. I want to go to the inn," Diana said, even though every fiber of her being was afraid. "Please go with the others now. If I see that the men do not believe me, I shall only then do what I must."

"I will not take my eyes off you," Silver Feather said. He gazed ahead at the inn, where the long front porch was lit by the glow of lanterns hung from the ceiling. There seemed to be enough light there, as well as what was left of early evening, to be able to see whatever transpired when Diana arrived.

"I shall go now," Diana said, her voice catching.

She took her hand from his. She smiled at him once again, then turned her eyes straight ahead and with a set jaw snapped the reins. Holding her chin high, she rode forward.

She could feel the eyes of her beloved on her all the way, even when she wheeled the stagecoach

up in front of the inn, where she received immediate attention.

She absently reached up and touched the brim
of her hat, which she had reclaimed from the cabin
where she had been held captive when they returned to the village.

She was glad to have the hat again at this pre-
carious moment in her life. A man came down the
steps and over to the stagecoach.

"Where in hell have you been?" he growled,
glancing back at the secured trunks, then at Diana
as she held the hat's brim low over her eyes.

"A wheel broke and came off," she said in as
manly a voice as possible. "It wasn't fixable. I had
to wait until someone came along. As you can see,
that took some time. Finally a man came by. He
had mercy and took me back to his place. It took
the blacksmith an ungodly amount of time to forge
the iron."

"I see it's fixed now," the man said, taking a
slow turn around the stagecoach, checking first
one wheel and then the next.

"Well," he said to Diana, "we all run into tough
luck sometimes. It's late. The shipment will be
taken to its destination tomorrow. For now, take
the stagecoach to the corral and unhitch the
horses. They need to be fed and watered and
rested before movin' on tomorrow. I'll see that the
stableboy takes care of 'em for you."

He glanced at the inn over his shoulder and

then at Diana. "And your room is ready," he said. "I saw to it that it was kept for you. I figured you'd run into some sort of trouble and would be tuckered out when you arrived here." He raked his eyes slowly over her. "Such a tiny man. I don't know how you manage this sort of work."

"I do just fine," Diana said, suddenly feeling nervous.

She drove the stagecoach to the corral where a boy helped her with the horses. She kept an eye out for the man, who had seemed a little too friendly. It always made her uneasy to have someone draw attention to her small frame. She wondered if they were weighing the possibility in their minds that she might be a female.

As the sun disappeared behind the distant hills, and everything around her lay in shadows, Diana walked from the corral toward the inn. The man who had met her was slowly rocking on the porch as he watched her every movement.

She felt a chill rush up and down her spine at the thought of him knowing about the ruse and playing along until he could pounce on both her and Silver Feather when the right opportunity offered itself to him.

Her insides tightened as she sauntered up the steps, pretending to have the slow gait of a man. She had learned to mock the masculine walk just for these kinds of moments when she was being closely scrutinized. Careful to keep the hat brim low, she glanced over at the man.

"Hiram's my name," he said, rising from the rocker. "Come on inside. I'll show you to your room. It's been ready for some time now, I guess you know."

"Sure do," Diana mumbled. "Sorry 'bout that, but a man can only do what a man can do, ain't that right?"

"Yep, guess so," Hiram said, walking into the inn with her. He pointed out the way to her room for the night.

"Second room on the left," he said, nodding down the hall.

Diana was glad that it was on the first floor. Her escape would be easily achieved.

"Do you want bathwater or food brought to your room, or would you rather go on to bed? You'll need to rest before you head out at daybreak tomorrow," Hiram said, walking her on to the room.

"Rest is more important to me than anything else right now," Diana said. "Anyhow, I only take one bath a week, if you know what I mean. Only sissies take baths more'n that."

The man threw his head back in a fit of laughter, then left her and went into a room opposite the hall from where she was supposed to spend the night. However, Silver Feather awaited her arrival. He would set up camp amid the trees. She planned to sleep with Silver Feather tonight. A warrior would wake her up before dawn, and she would hurry back to the room at the inn so no one would suspect that she'd not slept there.

Bone-tired, Diana eyed the bed wistfully. She wanted to fall upon it and go to sleep. But she needed to be with Silver Feather. It still seemed a miracle that they had found one another.

She stretched and yawned. Fighting off fatigue and hunger, she eyed the window. Her main goal now was to climb through it, go to the corral and get one of the horses from the stagecoach, and hurry to Silver Feather.

She knew they were both too tired to talk anymore tonight. But they could hold one another while they got some sleep. Tomorrow they would proceed with their plan.

Thus far, everything that she had told Hiram had been believable enough. She hoped so, anyway. That Hiram might have been lying through his teeth and was now waiting for her to flee into the darkness flitted through her mind, causing her to pause at the window. Diana scanned the shadowed landscape and saw nothing. Taking a deep breath, she threw a leg over the ledge and slid to the ground, then dashed to the corral.

She spied the stagecoach sitting unhitched near the barn. She only hoped that no one went out and inspected the cargo that still stood on top of it. If

they saw that there were rocks in the trunks . . .
No. She wouldn't think about that.

Hiram had seemed as tired as she was. He had
gone to his room. He hadn't mentioned the trunks,
nor did he seem concerned about their safety
through the night.

One of the stagecoach horses was grazing near
the fence. Diana reached out and stroked its muz-
zle, softly whispering to it, then unhitched the gate
and coaxed it out. Using the fence, she climbed
onto the horse and rode bareback to the road.

She rode for a little while, then saw Silver
Feather standing alongside the road just up ahead.
She went to him, drew a tight rein, and slid from
the horse into his arms.

They embraced, then kissed, Diana's knees
growing weak from the passion that swept
through her.

"Come with me," Silver Feather whispered
against her lips. "I have made a bed of blankets for
the two of us. All of my warriors but two are
asleep. The two that are awake will keep an eye
out for interlopers in the night. We shall be safe.
Diana, I see the weariness in your eyes."

"I have never been so tired," Diana said, her
voice breaking. "Oh, how I would rather sit and
talk with you until dawn, but, truthfully, I do need
to sleep."

"I have food from my parfleche for you before

we go to my blankets," Silver Feather said, knowing that she must be hungry.

"Thank you," Diana murmured as she gazed into his eyes, the moon's glow wafting through a break in the trees above them and allowing her to see him clearly. "Thank you for coming into my life again, too, Silver Feather. As it was, I just went along day by day doing what I must to survive. I had no one."

"You have me and my people now," Silver Feather said, leading her down onto a pallet of blankets.

He handed her some chunks of pemmican, and she gobbled it up, giggling afterward as she realized just how it must have looked to him, seeing her eat so hastily.

"I am anything but a lady tonight," she said, lowering her eyes.

He reached a hand to her chin and lifted it so they could see into one another's eyes. "You are all woman," he said huskily. "I want you so badly, Diana. Every bone in my body aches to have you. Since our last moments together, you have never left my heart. I missed you so. But now you are here with me. We have a second chance."

"After all of this is behind us, we shall do as we planned as children," Diana said, reaching a soft hand to his cheek. "We shall finally be married. I shall join you on a hunt and prove to you that I am truly your goddess."

"You are my goddess," he said, then twined his arms around her neck and drew her lips to his. "My Diana. My goddess."

They kissed and clung, then, both sighing with tiredness, stretched out together on the blankets.

Silver Feather placed a protective arm around her and held her close as their eyes shut.

"I love you so," Diana whispered to him. "I have always loved you."

"As I have loved you," Silver Feather said. Then both of them fell to sleep, finally together.

Horses neighed in the corral outside the inn, then fell silent again as the individual passed by and away into the darkness.

Shadows faded as morning drew nigh . . .

Chapter 16

Describe Adonis and the counterfeit
Is poorly imitated after you.
— William Shakespeare

Diana wanted to put all of this behind her so that she could begin her new life with Silver Feather. As unbelievable as it was to her, the plans she had made all those years ago would come to fruition. Thinking about her wedding day, Diana left the inn.

The rising sun had awakened her in time for her to get back to the inn before her absence was discovered.

She had made it to the room just in time for the knock on the door. Hiram had come to tell her the final destination.

She glanced quickly over at the bed, panic surging through her. It was evident that she had not slept there. One look at the room and Hiram would know that she had slept elsewhere.

"Just a minute," she said in her low voice.

"Keep your breeches on. I'm just steppin' into my drawers."

She hurried to the bed and threw back the blanket, pummeled the pillow, then went to the door.

As she opened it, she kept the brim of her hat low. "Hell's bells, ain't you in a rush," she mumbled. "Give a man time to get the sleep outta his eyes before comin' and draggin' him to only the good Lord knows where."

Diana sauntered from the room in her best practiced gait. "Where *are* we headed this mornin'?" she asked, walking beside Hiram down the corridor.

"I ain't goin' anywhere," Hiram said, looking straight ahead and not seeing that Diana gave him a questioning look. "I never planned to. And you're not going either. You can go back home and get your orders for your next stagecoach run."

"And I ain't goin' with the shipment? Why on earth not?" Diana asked, her insides tightening at the change in the plan.

"Plans have been changed, that's why," Hiram growled. He gave her a dark frown. "James Clawson, the one waitin' on the shipment, wired ahead last night and told me there was a change in the plan." He shrugged. "Don't matter none to me if I don't have to go on that uncomfortable stagecoach. I'll just head for home, where my sweetie awaits me."

"How are the trunks to be delivered, then, if not

by stagecoach?" Diana asked guardedly, walking alongside him through the lobby, where far to the left, in the dining area, many were sitting at tables covered by white linen tablecloths, sipping coffee and eating delicious-smelling food.

She fought off her hunger. The pemmican that she shared with Silver Feather last night and then again this morning would have to be enough until later. Diana shoved the thoughts away and concentrated on her predicament.

If several men came to escort the shipment, they might be enough to overpower Silver Feather and his warriors. Surely Silver Feather would not chance taking over the shipment and those who were delivering it to its final destination.

"By wagon," Hiram said, nodding a hello to a lovely lady who came past them in a beautiful, flouncy silk dress, her hair pulled atop her head in a tight bun.

Diana gazed over at him in time to see him wink flirtatiously at the lady, making her realize that not only did he have a role in stealing from the Choctaw, he also probably stepped out on the woman called his "sweetie."

They stepped out onto the wide porch just as a flash of lightning came from low-hanging, dark clouds. Diana flinched. That was all the Choctaw needed now—a storm. First a change in plans and now the threat of torrential rain to interfere in their plans to discover who was involved in stealing the bones.

"I wired my boss about the broken wheel on the stagecoach. He decided not to chance a repeat occurrence for the last leg of the journey north," Hiram said, waving to someone who had just come into sight from around the bend in the road. "And there he is now. Earl. Earl Sharp. The man who is going to take the shipment off your hands."

Diana went quiet when she saw the wagon approaching with a lone rider on the seat. She didn't think the wagon was much healthier than the stagecoach. But none of that mattered.

Seeing that only one man was in charge of delivering the trunks was a reprieve. That meant that overtaking him would be easy. But what was she to do with the damnable stagecoach? She *had* to ride away on it to make it look as though she still planned to take it back to New Town for a next shipment or Hiram and Earl would realize that something was awry.

The answer came quickly. She would wait for Earl to leave in the wagon, then after a short while, she would leave. She would make sure she was visible to either Earl or Hiram. Then at her first opportunity she would make a sharp right into the forest and hide the stagecoach.

She would take one of the horses from the team to use to catch up with Silver Feather. She'd unhitch the other horses and leave them to whoever might happen along. But hopefully no one would come before she and Silver Feather were long gone from the area.

"Mornin', Earl. Have an easy trip from New Town?" Hiram asked as the wagon came to a halt a few feet away.

"It was until now," Earl said, climbing down from the wagon. He looked heavenward, flinching when another flash of lightning lit the dark sky. "I hope this one moves on over. I don't like travelin' in an open wagon in the rain, especially with lightning bouncin' all around me."

"Now don't be a sissy, Earl," Hiram said, laughing throatily as he gazed at the thin, lanky man.

He then turned to Diana. "Go with Earl and help him unload the trunks onto his wagon," he said flatly. "Pronto!"

Diana nodded and walked to the corral, where the stagecoach still stood untouched.

She glanced over at the horses that she would soon be hitching to the stagecoach, mentally choosing which one would be the most dependable for her to ride after she got the stagecoach into hiding.

When one of the horses, a brown mare, made eye contact with her and whinnied, she knew that was the one. Almost mystically, it seemed to have read her mind. She hoped that everything else this morning would be as easy.

The man sidled the wagon up next to the stagecoach to make it easier to exchange the trunks from one place to the other.

Diana climbed atop the stagecoach, her eyebrows raising when Earl climbed onto the wagon.

"You hand 'em to me," he directed. "That is, if a tiny man like yourself can lift."

His eyes raked over her.

"Didn't eat many mashed taters when you were a kid, did'ja?" Earl teased, laughing.

"Never one much for taters," she managed in a low, scratchy tone. "Now let's get on with it. I've got things to do besides standin' here jawin' with you."

"Sure, sure," Earl grumbled.

Diana felt her spine stiffen and ache as she lifted first one trunk and handed it to Earl, then a second. She tried not to groan, even though the rocks in the trunk made it ungodly heavy. She did not want to reveal her discomfort.

"Ain't hankerin' to open these things when I get 'em delivered," Earl said, setting both trunks aside. He shuddered visibly. "Even one whiff'll probably make me puke."

Earl Sharp *knew* what he was going to be transporting on his wagon.

She had thought that perhaps he had been hired to just deliver, without knowing what he was handling. It seemed such knowledge wouldn't be shared with too many.

She wanted to ask the man just what his connection was to the bones, yet knew it wouldn't be wise. She would have to wait until later when Silver Feather and his warriors took possession of the wagon.

She could feel Silver Feather's eyes watching them even now and knew that he would be aware of the change in plans. He would know to follow the wagon. And he would have to know that she would find a way to join him as soon as possible.

"That's it," Earl said, jumping down from the wagon. He wiped his hands onto his denim breeches, then climbed aboard again, on the seat. "Thanks for helpin'."

He nodded a good-bye to Hiram and Diana, then snapped his reins and drove away.

Diana scrambled to get the six horses hitched to the stagecoach, relieved that Hiram had lost interest in her and had gone back inside, probably for a tall order of flapjacks and a cup of steaming hot coffee.

The thought of pancakes made her stomach growl again, but she fought off the hunger as she had been forced to fight off her need for sleep, rest, and food these past days.

"Soon it will all be done," she whispered to herself as she swung the horses out onto the road, the stagecoach teetering one way and then another as she sped away from the corral.

She kept her eye on the wagon as it lumbered

along the road, Earl unaware of the Indians following his progress.

Diana knew that Silver Feather wouldn't make a move just yet. He needed to put a few miles between the ambush and the inn. Diana had plenty of time to find a place to abandon the stagecoach before catching up with Silver Feather and his warriors, who she knew were hidden in the shadows of the trees.

A clap of thunder drew her attention, and she realized that it was more distant than before. She gazed heavenward and saw that the storm had raced overhead and was no longer a threat.

Sighing with relief, she drove onward, her eyes never leaving the wagon ahead of her. Once she was far enough away from the inn, she fell back some distance until the wagon was no longer in sight. Should the driver look over his shoulder, he wouldn't see her.

Scanning the side of the road, she found the perfect place. There was enough space for the stagecoach to enter, and enough shrubbery to hide it.

Hurrying along, she hid the stagecoach and detached the horses.

She glimpsed the shine of water through a break in the trees a short distance away. Some thick grass swayed near the water. This was a fine place to leave the horses until they were found.

Smiling, she patted each one and spoke soft words of apology to them, then hurried on to the brown mare, mounted her bareback, and rode away from the thick cover of trees.

Once she was out on the road again, she made certain that she didn't get close enough for Earl to catch sight of her.

Diana rode for some time, then slowed the horse to a lope when she saw what was transpiring up ahead. Silver Feather and his warriors had just made their move.

They had come from the forest and were now on each side of the wagon.

When she saw Earl's arms lift into the air as many arrows were aimed at him, Diana nodded her head.

"He deserves what he gets," she said to herself, then nudged her steed's flanks with the heels of her shoes and rode at a hard gallop until she wheeled to a stop beside Silver Feather.

"What the—?" Earl said as he stared at Diana, then gasped in disbelief as she yanked her hat off and her golden hair tumbled in thick waves past her shoulders to her waist.

"Why, you ain't a man at all," Earl said, his voice tight. "You're a—"

"A lady," Silver Feather said. "She is my woman."

"Diana," Diana replied. "Just call me Diana."

"You damn wench," Earl shouted, his eyes filled with rage. "You'll pay for this."

"No, I don't think so," Diana said, plopping the

hat back on her head and tucking her hair under it again. She was looking forward to the day when she would never wear the damnable hat again.

"Tell me where you are taking these trunks, and why," Silver Feather said, his eyes narrowed angrily, raising his bow a notch.

"I cain't," Earl mumbled. "They'll kill me."

"Would you rather die by arrow or bullets?" Silver Feather asked.

Earl swallowed hard. Sweat streamed from his brow. "If I had my choice, it'd damn well not be by an arrow."

"Then tell me everything," Silver Feather said tightly. "Everything!"

Chapter 17

*There was never any yet that wholly could
escape love, and never shall there
be any, never so long as beauty
shall be, never so long as eyes can see.*

— Longus

There was terror in Earl's eyes as he looked from Diana, then back to Silver Feather. "Do I have to tell you? If I do . . ."

"If you do not, you will die," Silver Feather said through clenched teeth. He motioned to his warriors, who were no longer on their horses, to step closer. Their bowstrings were also notched with deadly arrows.

Silver Feather lowered his own weapon and moved closer to the lanky man. He leaned down into Earl's face.

"Where are you taking the bones?" he asked flatly. "What do you want with them?"

"I didn't take the bones from the house," Earl stammered, his eyes wide as he gazed into Silver Feather's. "Come on. You're blamin' the wrong man. I—I only deliver 'em, nothin' else."

"You are no less guilty of the crime than those

who took the bones and those who are waiting for them," Silver Feather said, his eyes glaring. "Tell me now. Your time is running out."

Earl was frozen with fear as he took an unsteady step away from Silver Feather. He looked past him at Diana, then to the many arrows pointed directly at him. He knew that at any moment he could die.

"All right, I'll tell you," he said, his voice cracking with fear. "I was on my way to a factory. It's a secret location. Only those involved know about it."

He swallowed hard. "I am only the driver. I have no role whatsoever in turning the bones into buttons. But I've been sworn to secrecy. If my boss finds out I've tattled, I'll be horsewhipped, perhaps even killed. All the people involved in the operation, all who work in the factory, are sworn to secrecy. They get good pay for their labor."

Silver Feather and Diana were both in such shock that words would not come.

"The skulls are the most valuable," Earl gulped out. "They make the shiniest buttons . . . and combs."

As Earl rattled on, telling the horrible truth to a petrified audience, Diana suddenly felt sick to her stomach. What the man was saying about how bones were being used was so unreal and disgusting.

She recalled demanding fancy buttons on her gowns and dresses as a little girl, and how she had adored wearing fancy combs in her hair on special occasions.

Could they have been made from bones?

Silver Feather abhorred what the man was revealing. It took all his willpower not to kill Earl Sharp on the spot.

But he knew that the man was still needed. He had to lead the Choctaw warriors to the factory.

The evil white men must be stopped—forever.

Stiff and feeling a coldness in his heart, Silver Feather reached out and placed a hand at the man's throat.

He squeezed only slightly, yet it was enough to cause Earl to gasp and his eyes to bulge with fright.

"Please—" Earl squeaked out. "Please don't kill me. I told you everything that I know. Please have mercy on my soul!"

"Who has ever had mercy on my people?" Silver Feather hissed. "Now do you agree, or not, to take me to the factory?"

"Yes! Yes!" Earl said quickly, breathing more easily and rubbing his throat after Silver Feather took his hand away. "I'll take you. Times are hard and I need money, but I've always been disgusted by what those men are doing."

Not able to stand there anymore, Diana turned and ran behind a bush, hung her head, and vomited. Silver Feather hurried to her.

He laid his bow aside, and scooped a handful of

water from a creek flowing nearby, then gently washed Diana's mouth with it.

She broke into tears. "I can't believe people can be so heartless," she cried. "So insane! To actually—"

She couldn't say it. The thought of even saying what the bones were being used for caused the bitterness to rise once again into her throat.

She fought against throwing up again, then turned her sorrowful eyes up at Silver Feather.

"*I* am white," she said, her voice catching. "I—I feel so guilty to say that I am. White people are guilty of so much wrong against the red man. They steal from them, cheat them, kill them, and now this?"

Tears spilled from her eyes as Silver Feather looked at her with love and adoration. He reached out and wiped them away.

"Do not cry," he said softly.

He drew her into his arms. "You are not like them," he assured her. "Your heart is pure."

"My heart is bleeding for your people," she sobbed. "I cannot help but cry and feel such shame for all the terrible things that have been done to you and those you love."

She gazed up at him, searching his eyes. "I will do anything to help right all the wrongs," she said.

His feelings for Diana overwhelmed him. Silver Feather lowered his lips to hers. He kissed her softly and lovingly, then stepped away from her.

"Oh, Silver Feather, how I have missed you," Diana whispered.

"I waited for you, my woman. Somehow, deep within my heart, I knew that this moment would come. I knew you and I would be together again. How could it not happen, when our love for one another is so real and pure?" Silver Feather said, smiling at her.

"All of my life has led me to this moment," Diana said, returning his smile as he held her hands in his. "My love, I want nothing more than to be with you for the rest of my—of *our*—lives."

Silver Feather's eyes wavered. He took his hands from hers and turned to gaze at the wagon where the trunks awaited delivery. Then he looked into Diana's eyes once again.

"Perhaps you should not be a part of this," he said. He gently touched her face. "My woman, my sweet Diana, it will be dangerous."

"I have faced danger before and I'm still alive," she said. "Please? I wish to go with you. I want to help in whatever way that I can. What those men are doing is so darkly evil."

"I will allow you to go with me, then, but for only one reason," Silver Feather said. He eased his hand from hers. He bent to pick up his bow and slid it over his left shoulder. "I do not want you out of my sight ever again."

He twined his free arm around her waist, drew

her close, and kissed her again, then they walked back to where Earl Sharp was awaiting his fate.

His face had lost its color. He visibly trembled from head to toe as he gazed directly into Silver Feather's eyes. Silver Feather stepped up to him and glared back at him.

"And so what is next?" Earl stammered, glancing from Silver Feather to Diana, then back to Silver Feather.

"You will lead us to the factory and—"

The man suddenly interrupted him. "And then—what—of me?" Earl stammered, his eyes wild.

"For now you must stay with us as our captive," Silver Feather said tightly.

"I, personally, ain't never had nothing against redskins," Earl said. "I just have to do what I must to make money to survive. I have a wife. She's with child."

Diana was alarmed at this new information. If anything happened to this man, what then of the woman and child? She knew what it felt like to be alone in the world.

She looked quickly over at Silver Feather.

"If you do what you are ordered to do, you will be with your wife soon," Silver Feather said. "It should not take too long to accomplish my plan."

"How can you assure my safety?" Earl asked. "When it is discovered what I have done, my life won't be worth spit, nor will my wife's."

"The men who would cause you harm will be taken care of by the Choctaw," Silver Feather told him. "Just do what you must for us and you will earn your freedom."

"I will—I will—" Earl said, gulping hard. He humbly lowered his eyes. "Thank you."

"White Cloud, take a horse from those that pulled the wagon," Silver Feather said, giving him a stern gaze. "This will be his horse."

He looked at his other warriors. "Lead the other horses into the forest and secure them," he ordered. "We will return later and take them to our village."

"But what of the bones?" Earl asked.

Silver Feather chuckled. "The trunks carry rocks, not bones," he said. Earl's eyes widened in surprise. "The bones are where they belong—with the Choctaw people."

A horse was brought to Earl and he mounted it bareback.

"You will ride at my left side so that I can keep an eye on you," Silver Feather said, frowning at Earl. He smiled over at Diana. "My woman rides at my right."

"Your woman?" Earl said, shuddering with disgust. "You have referred to her more than once as yours, and you—you—treat her as though she is your wife. It's disgusting."

"Yes, a man such as you would think such a

thing," Silver Feather said bluntly. "But she will soon be my wife."

He flicked his reins and rode off, Diana alongside him. When Earl didn't move quickly enough, Silver Feather turned and gave him a threatening scowl.

Earl soon caught up to Silver Feather. "The factory is some distance away," he offered. "One night of camp must be made before we get there."

Silver Feather nodded and rode onward, stopping only long enough to share a quick meal of pemmican with Diana and Earl as they momentarily rested. His warriors ate a quick snack of the same, then all rode on. Only when Silver Feather became aware of the weariness in his woman's eyes did he decide that it was time to stop for the night.

He smiled at Diana as she caught him looking at her. He cherished the thought of what their future together would be.

He looked over at the weasel of a man and thought about what lay ahead at the factory.

"Where else have bones been gotten?" Silver Feather asked suddenly, drawing Earl's eyes quickly to him.

"From all over," Earl replied. "Some have been dug from the ground where Indian burial grounds were discovered. Some farmers have found bones as they prepared the earth to plant their crops. No matter if the bones are of those of white people or red, they are taken to the factory for buttons. But it is the bones taken from the Indian bone houses that are the most sought. Many have been found. Many."

Silver Feather's jaw tightened. He looked away from Earl quickly, before he could give in to his desire to reach over and hit him. Silver Feather found the willpower that kept him from doing as his heart desired.

The important thing was to get to that factory and destroy it before any more buttons or combs could be made from other tribes' bones and skulls!

Chapter 18

*O, for life of Sensations,
rather than thoughts!*
—John Keats

Frogs sang their songs along the banks of a close-by river. A loon cried eerily in the dark across the water, as the moon poured its silver sheen into it, and across the land.

"The night is so beautiful, so peaceful," Diana murmured, nestling close to Silver Feather as they sat on a blanket stretched out atop a thick bed of grass. "I love night songs. They take me back to when I was a child and gazed from my open bedroom window, thinking of you and wondering if you were hearing the same songs as me."

"You were never off my mind," Silver Feather said, turning to her, their eyes meeting in the moonlight. "My Diana, are you truly here with me? Or are you a figment of my imagination? So often, through the years, I sat like this beneath the moon and stars, envisioning you beside me. At times I reached out to touch you, only to bring myself back to reality and feel sadness all over again."

"I am not a figment of your imagination tonight," Diana said, moving to her knees so that she was directly before him. She reached out to touch his face. "Nor are you of mine. My Silver Feather, ah, my Silver Feather. I am so glad that you are here—that you are aliv—"

"Shh," he said softly. "Do not say it."

He placed a gentle hand over her mouth and silenced what she had been about to say. Slowly his fingers glided over her soft lips before he took his hand away.

"It is so good to be sitting here with you tonight," he said thickly. "Did you get your fill of meat? Do you feel fresh and clean after our swim in the river?"

"Yes, to both things," Diana said, remembering the swim they took, far away from the eyes of the others, while two rabbits had slowly cooked over the campfire, the tantalizing aroma wafting out to them.

After Diana and Silver Feather's private swim, they went to join the others beside the campfire to enjoy the meal.

The captive had been untied long enough to eat, then tethered to a tree as the others stretched out on their blankets.

It was then that Diana and Silver Feather had

gone back to sit beside the river, far enough away so that they could have a full night of privacy.

"The rabbit tasted much better than pemmican," Diana said, making a face at the memory of that food.

"Pemmican is carried with us Choctaw at all times," Silver Feather said. He reached a hand to Diana's hair and slowly ran his fingers through the long golden tresses. "It is something that keeps us fed when there is no time to prepare other foods. It has kept many a red man alive while forced to be away from their homes long lengths of time."

"Then I shall be sure to learn how to make pemmican, so that my husband will always have food with him when he is forced to be away from me," Diana said.

"I will not like leaving you, even when I must go on the hunt with my brothers," Silver Feather said. "I want you with me at all times. I cannot bear to think that something—or someone—might take you away from me again."

"I am no longer that small child who was not in control of her own destiny," Diana said, her voice breaking. "I am a grown woman now, and my destiny is what I make it."

"No one will ever force anything on you again, or tell you what you can or cannot do," Silver Feather said, stroking her cheek with his fingertips. "And your destiny and mine are the same, are they not?"

"Yes, the same," Diana murmured as he wrapped his arms around her waist and drew her closer.

His lips found hers. He gave her a long, deep kiss, then his fingers went to the buttons of her shirt and began unfastening them.

"What are you doing?" Diana whispered against his lips. Her heart began pounding furiously in her chest.

She trembled as he slid a hand inside her shirt and found a breast. She sucked in a wild breath and threw her head back with rapture when his hand cupped her breast and his thumb circled her warm brown nipple. No man had ever touched her body.

When she had begun to have the feelings of a woman, she would close her eyes and envision Silver Feather touching her as he did. She had felt shame for such thoughts then.

But now, she felt only sheer ecstasy and a hunger within her that she had never felt before in her entire life.

It was a strange sort of ache at the juncture of her thighs—strange yet somehow delicious!

"Do you wish for me to stop?" Silver Feather asked, drawing her eyes back to his. "Is it too soon for me to be doing this? We have only just found each other again after such a long time. Do you truly still feel the same for me now, as you did those long years ago?"

"That, and more," Diana said, her voice sounding strange to her as passion coursed through her. "Oh, Silver Feather, I want to share everything with you. Until now, there were only my dreams. But now, you are truly here with me!"

"Are you saying that you want to make love?" Silver Feather asked, needing total reassurance. "I sense that you are feeling the same need as I. Am I right?"

"Yes, yes," Diana sighed, then melted inside when he threw open her shirt, bent low, and flicked his tongue over the nipple that was already tender from his caress.

She reached her hands to his hair and twined her fingers through the thick black locks, bringing him even closer to her. Her pulse raced as he licked his way around the nipple, then sucked it between his teeth and gently nibbled.

"Lord . . ." Diana whispered, her face aflame with desire.

Suddenly he was no longer touching or kissing her body. She didn't feel him anywhere.

Diana panicked, thinking that perhaps she had been too brazen by allowing him such intimacies, considering that they were truly still somewhat strangers to one another.

But she was wrong.

When she opened her eyes, she saw him standing before her, the moon's glow in the river a backdrop to what he was doing.

He had undressed down to his breeches, and as she watched breathlessly, he even removed them.

He stood like an Adonis, all muscle and copper. His hair hung long and thick to his waist, his midnight eyes reached inside her heart and called out to her.

"Diana, stand and undress," he said huskily.

Diana's eyes had only now dropped lower and found that part of him she hadn't seen since he was a young boy. But tonight, as she gazed at Silver Feather and saw how God had blessed the man, her knees grew weak.

They were so weak, they hardly held her up as she stood and started undressing as Silver Feather watched.

First she tossed her shirt aside, noticing how his eyes fell upon her breasts, as though caressing them. It was as if his tongue and lips were there again, causing her breasts to tingle so strangely.

And then she unfastened her breeches.

As she placed her thumbs at the waist and slowly began lowering them, she knew that her practice of not wearing underwear would expose her quickly to this man she loved. The prospect made her heart throb inside her chest so hard that she felt dizzied by it.

Dropping her breeches, she watched as his eyes moved down to the soft, golden tendrils of hair. She was more aware of that place now than ever before in her life.

There was an odd sort of throbbing, an ache.

Silver Feather came to her as she stepped out of her breeches and swept his arms around her waist. He drew her against him, and Diana could feel that sensual part of him against her body as he brought his lips hard against hers and kissed her.

Breathing hard, and heady from the building ecstasy, Diana twined her arms around his neck and strained her body against his.

She found herself being lowered to the blankets.

After she was stretched out beneath Silver Feather, his muscled body blanketing hers, Diana gasped with an intense passion when she felt his manhood probing where she so unmercifully throbbed.

"I shall be gentle," Silver Feather whispered against her lips. "The pain shall be brief, and then, my Diana, you will fly with me into the heavens."

Diana stiffened at the warning about pain. She knew nothing about lovemaking or what to expect. But his reassurance that the pain would be brief was enough for her to know that it would be. Silver Feather was not a man to lie.

"Just love me," she whispered against his lips. "I love you so much."

She trembled with readiness as she clung to his neck, and when she felt him pushing himself slowly into her, she felt a mixture of many things, but most of all, an intense love—such as she had never felt before.

Tonight, it was all so much more than two children laughing and running, or riding horses together, when they had known those years ago that they should not be together.

Tonight they were discovering their true feelings for one another, that which no man could take away!

Silver Feather held her gently as he continued to fill her. When he found the barrier that he had expected, he paused.

"Now is the time," he whispered against her lips. "Cling tightly to me. The pain will be brief. Then let yourself go, Diana. Feel what I feel. Embrace it!"

"Yes, I will," she said, truly trembling now, not so much from anticipation but from the endearing love she had felt for him from the beginning of time.

She felt a brief sting of pain, and then everything within her became like liquid velvet as the pleasure side of this thing called lovemaking claimed her.

She had never envisioned anything could be this wonderful, this beautiful.

She clung to him as their bodies moved together, hers seeming to know what to do without being taught.

As he kissed her, with a hot and demanding mouth, she returned the kiss in kind. She wrapped her legs around him and felt him going even more deeply within her. She clung.

They moved.

They kissed.

They groaned.

And then suddenly it was as though all heaven had opened up and taken them in as the most wondrous of feelings overwhelmed Diana and Silver Feather simultaneously.

They moaned against each other's lips as their bodies shook and quivered.

And then it was finished, and they lay still, holding one another.

"You felt it, did you not?" Silver Feather whispered against her cheek, his heart pounding from the pure pleasure he had just experienced with the woman he had always loved.

"And more," Diana said, her eyes searching his. She stroked his cheek. "Silver Feather, I never knew such a feeling existed. I—I had always loved being with you, but tonight it was utter joy and bliss. I love you, Silver Feather. Oh, how I love you."

"My woman, my love," Silver Feather whispered, softly kissing the hollow of her throat.

Chapter 19

For thee the wonder-working earth
puts forth sweet flowers.
                                    —Lucretius

The next leg of the journey was softened for Diana
by memories of the night and how she had discovered the wonders of making love with a man—not
just any man, but Silver Feather.

It was a miracle that she was with him again, a
miracle that brought a song to her heart.

She glanced over at him and saw how tall he sat
in the saddle, his muscles so evident beneath the
tight buckskin shirt.

She trembled even now at how it had felt to be
held by those strong arms and how wonderful it
had been to have his lips against hers. And then
had come the marvelous moment when they
soared into the heavens together as their love for
one another had been fulfilled.

Diana hadn't wanted to part from him, so he
had held her the entire night as they slept. When

she had awakened this morning, she had not wanted to leave their love nest.

She wished they could have stayed there forever, just the two of them beside the river.

But Silver Feather was on a mission, and she was there to help him in any way that she could. The knowledge of the plan for using the stolen bones turned her heart icy cold.

Diana looked ahead and knew that they didn't have much farther to go. Earl had explained the day's journey to Silver Feather as they sat beside the morning fire, eating the meat of the rabbits that had been caught by one of Silver Feather's warriors before Diana and Silver Feather had awakened. Since then, they had traveled steadily, stopping only to rest for a short while, to drink from a fresh stream and eat handfuls of berries that they had found growing in the thickets.

"We are almost there," Earl said, breaking through Diana's thoughts. He sidled his horse closer to Silver Feather's and pointed to a long, low building made of logs that sat back from the road. "I was to drop off the shipment of bones at that building."

Silver Feather nodded.

The man rode away from Silver Feather again, as Diana moved closer. She followed Silver Feather's gaze and saw what he was seeing.

Smoke spiraled from three chimneys on top of the building. Three wagons were lined up outside the one large door at the front. Wooden boxes were being carried out and loaded onto the wagons.

Diana could only surmise that buttons were in those boxes.

"What are you going to do now?" Diana asked, drawing Silver Feather's eyes to her. "I—I can't help but be afraid for you, Silver Feather, no matter what you do."

"It must be done," he said, his voice drawn. "And I have brought enough warriors to see that it is."

"But *what*?" Diana asked, fingers of fear running down her spine. "What are you going to do?"

"Whatever it takes to stop this," Silver Feather replied. He reached over and gently touched her cheek. "I would rather you not get involved, yet I do not want you to stay where I am not, either. I want to make certain that you are not harmed in any way."

"Please don't worry about me," Diana answered. "I have learned how to take care of myself. Just go ahead and do what must be done. I promise that I will stay close. I will do whatever I can to help."

Silver Feather leaned low, reached inside his saddlebag, and brought a pistol out of it. Diana's eyes widened when she recognized it as one of hers. She gazed into Silver Feather's eyes, smiled, then gladly took it.

"You will need this if I cannot be there to protect you," he said. "Be careful, my woman. Be careful."

"I shall," she said, relishing the feel of the pistol in her hand.

"My warriors, listen well," Silver Feather said, wheeling his horse around to face them. "Each of you has his own duty to perform today. To achieve our goal, we must see our task to fruition. The important thing is to be careful so that you may greet your wives and children upon our arrival home."

He motioned toward the loaded wagons just outside the building. "Those who have been assigned to take the bones, go," he said. "Stop the men who drive the wagons. Take them to our Choctaw village. Lock them up. They will be taken care of later."

As he continued to give orders, Diana grew more and more afraid. She was terrified of how this might end. If Silver Feather took hostages, he could bring trouble to his people.

But she wouldn't interfere again. Silver Feather was an intelligent man. He had surely thought it all out very carefully before acting.

Silver Feather watched as some of his warriors broke away from the others and rode in a cloud of dust toward the departing wagons.

Diana rode with Silver Feather and the warriors

assigned to stay with him. As they reached the
building, they hurriedly surrounded it just as his
other warriors overtook the wagons and forced the
white men from them.

"Come with me and Diana," Silver Feather said
to the remaining warriors as he quickly dismounted.

With arrows notched on their bows, Silver
Feather and his warriors rushed into the building,
catching everyone inside it off guard. Diana followed closely behind with her pistol drawn.

Panic came into the eyes of the white men and
women who stood before long rows of tables
where they had been carving buttons.

None of them had had the chance to draw a
weapon. They were surrounded by the Choctaw
warriors, the arrows threateningly close to them
all.

Diana shivered inwardly when she saw tables
of skulls, and farther down, the combs that came
from them. Buttons made from the bones were
stacked along the back of the tables, ready to be
put in boxes for shipping.

"Who is in charge?" Silver Feather shouted as
he tried not to stare at the stacks of bones that were
awaiting their fate.

There was no response.

There was only fear in the eyes of the workers,
who stood looking guardedly back at the Indians
and questioningly at Diana.

Diana moved closer to Silver Feather. "Look for the men dressed more expensively than the others," she said softly. "Look for those who were obviously not working. They would be the ones in charge. The poorly clothed ones are the laborers."

Silver Feather and several of his warriors walked along the rows of people, and one by one, those who were dressed expensively were found and rounded up.

Although those men tried to lie their way out of what they feared was about to happen to them, Silver Feather ignored their pleas and ordered them to be tied up and led from the building.

"The rest of you file out, one by one!" Silver Feather shouted, his arrow still notched to his bow, ready to be released at anyone who might try to run or attack the warriors.

"Please don't kill us," one of the men begged as he walked outside with the others. "We are here only to make money. If you let us go, we promise not to tell a soul that you were here."

Others spoke up, agreeing. The women nodded frantically, their eyes filled with tears.

Remembering being held "captive" by Diana's evil stepfather those many years ago, Silver Feather nodded.

"Go," he said gruffly. "You will not go to the authorities and tell them what has transpired here. What you were doing goes against all laws of nature and man. You should hang your heads in disgrace and shame."

Some did hang their heads in obvious shame, and the women began to cry again.

"Go!" he shouted. "Now! Or I might change my mind and cause you to suffer the same fate as those men who were just taken away."

Diana was not surprised by his kindness, for she had always known the goodness of his heart. She only hoped that this time it did not come back to haunt him. If just one of those people who were now scurrying out of the factory told anyone about what was happening, all of this could backfire and Silver Feather and his people could be endangered once again.

She quietly prayed as they followed the workers out of the building that he would get the chance to finally right this wrong that had been done to his Eagle Clan.

Silver Feather turned and gazed at the long building, then at Diana. "Come with me."

He took her hand.

Together they went back inside, where the bones lay piled along the tables. They walked slowly up and down the long rows where the remains awaited their fate.

Silver Feather stepped away from Diana and went to a large pile of buttons. He grabbed a handful, then angrily threw them across the room. He did the same with the combs.

"I'm so sorry," Diana murmured as she went to his side. "My love, I wish that I could do something."

"I have something to do myself," Silver Feather said, his jaw tight, his eyes filled with an intense anger that Diana had never seen before.

"What are you going to do?" Diana asked quietly. He didn't respond, but instead walked back outside. Diana went with him and stood aside as he shouted orders to his warriors.

"Set fire to the building!" he cried. "There is no way to return those bones and skulls to their rightful resting places. I have no idea where they came from. But the smoke from the bones will reach into the heavens. That is where it belongs!"

Several of the expensively dressed captives stepped closer to Silver Feather, their hands tied behind their backs.

"No!" one of them begged. "Don't burn them. So much money will go up in smoke!"

Silver Feather glared at the man, then helped to make torches, which were set aflame. Some were tossed inside. Others were tossed onto the roof.

As flames roared skyward, Diana shivered. She believed that she could see faces in those flames.

Silver Feather turned on his heel and approached the best-dressed man. He grabbed him by his throat. "Where did those bones and skulls come from?" he asked, his teeth clenched. "Who brought them here?"

"We have people everywhere scouting for burial grounds," the man gasped, his face reddening as he tried to get his breath.

Silver Feather recalled Earl Sharp saying the same thing.

"Farmers contact us about the bones they turn up as they prepare their gardens," the man choked out. He tried to swallow. "It doesn't matter whose bones they are. Bones are bones. But—the skulls are the most favored of all. The combs—"

"Enough!" Silver Feather cried as he dropped his hand from the man's throat. "I have heard enough!"

He slapped the man so hard across his face that the man's body lurched, then fell backward, onto the ground.

Silver Feather glared at him, then reached down and grabbed him up and shoved him hard toward the corral at the far side of the factory. The rest of the men were taken there and forced onto horses.

Then Silver Feather went to Diana. He gazed softly into her eyes as he framed her face between his hands.

"Let us go home now," he said somberly. "Our job is finished here."

She wanted to ask what his plans were for the captives, but she chose not to. She wasn't sure that she wanted to hear the answer.

Although she knew that these men deserved

whatever fate awaited them, she hoped it wouldn't be too severe, for she was afraid that Silver Feather might regret a harsh judgment. If the white authorities came to his village, they might take him and his warriors away to imprison them or order them onto reservations.

Either place was hell for the red man!

Chapter 20

Lo, this is she that was the
world's delight.
—Algernon Charles Swinburne

A campfire burned in the distance, giving light where night had fallen with its black shroud. Stars twinkled like diamonds in the velvet sky, the moon a silver ball overhead as Silver Feather rested on his knees beside a stream, washing his hands over and over in the clear water.

Diana sat on a blanket near him. They had left the campsite, where meat cooked slowly over a fire. The wind even now brought with it the smell of meat cooking and the sound of voices talking over the day's events.

All but a few had gone on to the village, where the evil ones would be locked away until Silver Feather arrived to order their final fate.

Diana felt so much for Silver Feather at this moment. It was a combination of an intense love and a sadness that came with the knowledge of how he felt about his discovery. So many of the bones came from tribes who might never know about their ancestors' graves having been desecrated.

"I cannot seem to get the smell of the burning bones off my flesh," Silver Feather said, looking at Diana. His hands were sore from his repeated scrubbing of them. "It clings, just as the memory of what those evil men were doing will remain in my aching heart."

"But you stopped them," Diana said, moving closer to him. "They will pay." She rested a gentle hand on his arm. "And what you have done is so noble. So many souls are finally at peace tonight, and all because of you."

"Had I only known earlier, I could have—" he began, but stopped when she pressed a finger to his lips.

"Shhh," she murmured. "Please do not feel that you have failed. You had no idea such a thing was happening. Had you not gone to your sacred bone house, it would have continued."

"I was drawn there by my dreams," Silver Feather said, sitting down by Diana on the thick grass beside the stream. He slowly wiped his hands dry on his buckskins. "When I had more than one dream about my people's sacred bone house, I knew that I must go there. I thought I was being drawn there to pray. Instead, I was being warned about what was about to transpire."

"You have done so much today," Diana said. "Once the word spreads of what those men were doing, others like you will seek out more of those who are participating in this horrendous industry. Eventually, it will be stopped."

"If only I had known sooner," Silver Feather repeated, hanging his head, running his fingers through his thick black hair in frustration.

Their private campfire burned low behind them. Silver Feather stood and held a hand out to Diana.

"I'm glad your men understand your need for privacy tonight," Diana said, sitting beside Silver Feather close to the fire on the blanket that they had spread out.

She looked through a thin screen of willow branches hanging low behind her and Silver Feather and saw the other fire. "I will go soon and get some of the meat for our evening meal."

She scooted close to his side, nestling against him. "But first, I want some more time with you like this. I'm not all that hungry, are you?"

"My appetite was swept away some time ago," Silver Feather replied. "I am not certain when it will return. I am afraid that when I eat, I will taste the bitterness of what has happened to the bones of not only my people but so many others."

"Yes, I know," Diana said, swallowing hard.

She closed her eyes as she tried to fight off the memory of the raging flames at the factory. She remembered the ghostly images spiraling heavenward.

"My woman, your eyes are closed, and I just saw you shiver," Silver Feather said, reaching for another blanket and placing it around her shoulders. "You are cold. I shall warm you."

Diana opened her eyes and gazed into his. "It was not the cold that caused me to shiver," she said, her voice breaking. "It was the memory of what I saw in the flames and smoke as the factory burned."

"Yes, I saw it, too," Silver Feather said, drawing her closer, hugging her. "In time, that memory will fade. All will be well again."

"Not until the men who did this are made to pay," Diana said. "What are you going to do with them? There are several." She searched his face.

"I had first thought I would take them into New Town, but I have changed my plan," Silver Feather said. "For now they are being taken to my village, where they will be held captive until I return there." Silver Feather gazed into the flames, then turned to Diana again. "I will send for the sheriff in New Town," he said. "He can come and get the captives himself. As badly as I would like to hand down those men's sentences, I know that I should not. The white man's law differs from Choctaw law. It is best that their law determine the fate of those men who wronged so many."

"But what of other businesses elsewhere where buttons and combs are being made?" Diana asked.

"We know there must be others. Surely the captives know of others."

"They will be questioned, but if they do not reveal the other locations, I can only pray that more people like myself will step in and stop it elsewhere," he said, his voice drawn. "Or perhaps the white authorities will discover the evil they do and help weed them out, eventually stopping all those who practice such evil against mankind. Anything as vile and wrong as this cannot go on unpunished."

Again Diana could not help but think about all of the buttons that she had loved on her dresses. Surely some of them had been made from Indian bones. And the combs she had so proudly worn in her hair! She shivered at the thought of what they might have been made from.

She turned to Silver Feather.

"You may not have an appetite for food, but perhaps you hunger for other things?" she murmured, blushing at how bold she was at this moment.

Hearing what she was suggesting made Silver Feather's eyes turn to her. Then he looked into the distance.

He had purposely chosen this spot, far enough from the camp of his warriors that he could have privacy with his woman. He knew that being with her would help take away the sadness inside his heart, if only for the moment.

"Are you saying that you wish to make love?" he asked, smiling into Diana's eyes.

She blushed, lowered her eyes momentarily, then slowly looked up at him again. "Am I brazen to even suggest it?" she whispered. Her eyes danced into his. "Do you see me as . . . a hussy?" she then asked, giggling.

"A hussy?" Silver Feather said, forking an eyebrow. "I am not familiar with that word. Tell me its meaning."

"If you do not know the meaning, then you cannot see me in that light," Diana answered, lifting a soft hand to his cheek. "But I shall tell you anyway. It is a woman whom men see as loose—who gives up her body too easily to men."

"Then you are no hussy, or loose," Silver Feather said. He took her hand from his face and turned her so that she was on her back, then leaned down over her.

He moved closer to her, and as his hands crept up under her shirt, seeking the soft lobes of her breasts, he flicked his tongue across her lips, then lowered his mouth fully to hers and gave her a passionately hot kiss.

His thumbs circled her nipples, and Diana gasped with pleasure against his lips. He bent low over her and flicked his tongue across one breast and then the other.

Silver Feather felt the heat rising within him. His heart pounded so hard it felt like hammers inside his chest. While he was with Diana, it was so easy to forget everything but how she made him feel.

With quick, eager fingers, he lowered her breeches.

Full of anticipation, Diana kicked them away from her, then breathlessly gazed at Silver Feather as he stood above her and undressed.

A loon sang its eerie song across the water. Another loon, surely its mate, answered from far beyond the stream. Crickets sent their music across the land, as frogs echoed their love songs from the banks of the stream.

"My love," Silver Feather said throatily as he came to Diana and blanketed her with his powerfully muscled body.

When he kissed her this time, his mouth was hot and demanding.

He crushed her against him so hard that she gasped from the yearning that was building within her. She was feverish with desire as wild pleasure pumped through her veins.

"I love you so much," she whispered against his lips as he slid his mouth from hers and pressed his cheek against hers.

She twined her fingers through his long, thick hair as passion overwhelmed her.

"Love me now," she whispered against his cheek. "Please."

He leaned away from her. His eyes were dark with desire as he gazed down at her.

He placed a gentle hand at her cheek, then swept it down and cupped her breast.

"You are the only woman I ever wanted," he said, his voice breaking. "From the time we were innocent and young, I knew even then that I would have no one but you for my wife."

She flung her arms around his neck. "We are together for eternity. Love me, Silver Feather. Oh, please make love with me now, or I might burst from need."

He brought his lips down onto hers in a gentle kiss, before it became hot and passionate as he plunged himself fully into her and began his rhythmic thrusts. Her body responded to him as she lifted her hips high to receive him more deeply within her.

Silver Feather's head began to reel as the pleasure mounted within him. His arms snaked around her and he held her more closely, reveling in her soft, creamy flesh against his.

Overcome with love, Diana gave a cry of pure, sweet agony as she felt the fever build within her.

She slid her legs around him and rode him, thrusting up against him as he came to her with his own strokes.

"My woman, my love," Silver Feather whispered into her ear. "Now, my woman. Now!"

"Yes, now!" she cried to the heavens, clinging to

him as lovely stars seemed to burst forth from the sky.

Her whole body seemed fluid with fire as they found their ultimate pleasure. Then, breathing hard, she lay beside the fire in Silver Feather's arms.

"I am still amazed at how wonderful it is," she whispered against his cheek, as she ran her hands slowly down his muscled back, over his hip and around his body until she felt that part of him that had just taken her to paradise.

Silver Feather leaned to one side as she stroked him, watching his face as he closed his eyes and enjoyed another moment of bliss.

When he reached that plateau again, Diana watched his body quake, spilling his seed. He emitted a deep sigh of wonder. Then his eyes opened and he smiled into hers.

"What you just did—" he said, laughing softly as he took her hand away from him and wiped it clean on the corner of the blanket.

"You enjoyed it so much," Diana said, surprised that he had taken such pleasure in what she had just done.

"You can get pleasure as well when I am not in you," he said, stroking her womanhood.

Diana closed her eyes and lay back until she, too, found that exquisite place as he caressed her into a wonderful and long climax.

When it was over, she opened her eyes and

gazed at him, her body still trembling, while the place he had caressed still throbbed.

"It did feel the same," she said, searching his eyes.

"There are many ways to make love with the one you love," Silver Feather said, stretching out beside her and holding her close.

Diana clung to him for a moment, then laughed softly. "I am so hungry now," she said, sitting up and smiling down at him. "In fact, I feel ravenous."

Silver Feather chuckled. He reached for her clothes and handed them to her. They hurriedly dressed, then Silver Feather reached for her.

"Let us go now and eat with the others," he said. "Suddenly I feel lightened of all my burdens."

"I'm so glad," Diana said, walking beside him, barefoot, in the soft, damp grass of night.

She held his hand as they moved toward the beckoning fire, where the smell of cooked meat permeated the air.

She glanced over at Silver Feather. Beneath the moonlight, she could tell that he was different since their lovemaking. The tension was gone around his mouth, and his jaw was no longer tight.

She was so glad that she had been able to lift his burden, at least for the moment.

But when they arrived at his village, it would all start over again. He would come eye to eye with those men who were responsible for the desecration. She would be glad when those men were gone.

"Soon we will be married," Silver Feather said, smiling over at her. "After all of this is behind us."

"Then I shall finally be your Goddess of the Hunt!" she said, smiling broadly at him.

"You already are," he said, returning her smile. "You are my goddess of everything."

"I love just being yours," she said, giggling.

Chapter 21

Dawn was just breaking along the horizon when Diana awakened and quickly realized where she had slept.

They had arrived at Silver Feather's village late last night.

It had been much too late to send for the sheriff, who would surely take the men into custody after hearing about the sort of evil they were guilty of perpetrating.

Diana turned onto her right side and smiled as she reached out to touch the impression of Silver Feather's body that still dented the plush feather mattress.

She knew his plans for this morning, so she understood why he hadn't awakened her. He had sent a scout ahead to New Town to explain about the prisoners to the sheriff. She expected the prisoners to be gone from the village soon.

She gasped with surprise when she saw a doe-skin dress, embellished with beautiful beads, spread out on a bench along the far wall. Moccasins rested on the floor underneath the bench. She knew they had been placed there for her.

Silver Feather knew that Diana wouldn't want to put on the terrible breeches and shirt again. She threaded her fingers through her golden hair to remove the tangles and hurried to the dress.

She ran her palm across the softness of the fabric, already knowing how it would feel against her skin. It would be pure heaven compared to what she had been forced to wear in order to look like a man as she drove the stagecoach.

Excited at the prospect of wearing such a beautiful dress, she tugged off the old flannel shirt she had used as a nightgown the evening before.

They had gone to the nearby river, bathed in the moonlight, and then gone to bed, too tired to make love again. It had been wonderful just to snuggle up next to him on the soft mattress and to fall asleep there.

The doeskin dress slid on easily, and her feet slipped into the moccasins. Diana twirled around delightedly. She felt like a Choctaw princess!

Eager to see Silver Feather, she left the bedroom with quick steps. When she came to the main room of the cabin, she stopped and looked slowly around her, surveying how the man she loved lived.

Silver Feather's cabin was furnished simply. Two rocking chairs sat before the huge stone fireplace that stretched across one end wall. There were also a couch, another chair, and tables where kerosene lamps sat, their chimneys black with soot.

She turned and gazed into another room, which she knew was the kitchen. From where she stood, she could see a table and two chairs, a cookstove, and several other tables that she assumed were preparation tables. She could also see that fresh food had been brought in and placed on one of the tables.

She recognized corn, squash, peppers, chives, muscadines, and herbs.

Cook pots hung from hooks on the ceiling, just above the table.

"This is your home now," Silver Feather said as he came up behind Diana, startling her.

She turned and smiled at him as he swept an arm around her waist and drew her against his hard body. Today he wore only a breechclout and moccasins.

"My home," Diana murmured. "It has been so long since I have had a true home."

"You can make of this house whatever you wish," Silver Feather said, brushing a kiss across her brow.

"This cabin is fine the way it is now, but—"

"But?" Silver Feather asked, his eyes dancing.

"But I shall want to put *some* pretty things around the rooms, if you truly don't mind," Diana murmured. "I look forward to living with my feminine side again. I might want to place some lacy things here and there. May I?"

"As I said, you can make of this house whatever you want, for it is now also yours," Silver Feather said, then visibly stiffened as they both heard the sound of horses entering the village.

"They have arrived," he said, stepping away from Diana. He went to the door, stopped, and turned to her. "Come. Be a witness to what happens today to those men who wronged my people and so many others."

"I'll be glad to," Diana said, lifting the hem of the beautiful dress and hurrying to him. "I shall be proud to stand at your side as you send them into captivity."

He took her hand, and they stepped out into the morning sunlight together.

Sheriff Chance Duffy drew a tight rein close to them, his pale gray eyes moving slowly over Diana and then stopping on Silver Feather as two other white men rode up to join him. The badges on their jackets picked up the shine of the sun and reflected it into Diana's eyes.

"My deputies, Klein and James," Sheriff Duffy

said, motioning with a gloved hand toward the two men.

"And this is Diana, who will soon be my wife," Silver Feather said.

The sheriff tipped his hat to her, yet it was evident in his eyes that he did not approve of the relationship. No white man ever approved of a white woman marrying a man with copper skin. It was taboo. It was forbidden.

But this was Diana's life, and no man would dictate to her about how it should be. She was proud to stand at her beloved's side, no matter the color of his skin.

Ignoring the sudden contempt that he saw in the sheriff's eyes, Silver Feather stepped away from Diana. He went to the sheriff and raised a hand for a handshake. He was aware that the sheriff hesitated, but Silver Feather held his hand out until the sheriff shook it.

After the handshake, Sheriff Duffy dismounted, as did his two deputies.

"I hear you've rounded up a bunch of hooligans that need seeing to," Sheriff Duffy said, glancing over his shoulder as White Cloud went to the small cabin and opened the door.

Diana watched the men stumble out of the cabin, shielding their eyes from the bright sun.

"You have been told what they are guilty of, have you not?" Silver Feather said, turning and watching the men being ushered toward him.

"Yes. A horrendous thing it is, too," Sheriff Duffy said somberly. "I had heard about this sort of thing happening, but no one could prove it. No man has the right to take the bones of the dead from where they were buried—especially not to use them for making buttons and combs. I will gladly see to their punishment. We can't have men going around this countryside digging up bones of the dead, desecrating graves."

He visibly shuddered. "Disgusting," he said. "Utterly disgusting."

"In my case, the men did not dig my people's bones," Silver Feather said flatly. "They went to our people's sacred bone house and took the remains from there."

"I was told that you have the bones back in your possession," Sheriff Duffy said, pulling a cigar from an inside jacket pocket, slamming it into his mouth.

"Yes, and our bone house will be rebuilt," Silver Feather said tightly. "The bones will be back where they belong."

The sheriff lit his cigar, dropped the match to the ground, and stamped the flame out with the heel of his boot, then nodded. "And these are all of the guilty ones, eh?" he said, the cigar sliding to the corner of his mouth.

Diana gave Silver Feather a questioning glance, for as yet Silver Feather had not mentioned Harry Braddock and his role in this. She wondered why.

He hadn't even talked to her about him. She had just assumed that he would send the sheriff to Dettro Manor to collect him as well.

And would there be a mention of the young man who had begged to be let go because of "family," who had already been sent away, to return to his home?

No. She doubted that he would ever be mentioned again.

But Harry Braddock?

"This is it," Silver Feather said, his jaw tight. "And thank you for being understanding about the plight of my people. I appreciate your kindness.

Sheriff Duffy frowned at the prisoners. He nodded to his two deputies. "Tie them so they will follow us on foot to New Town," he ordered. "No need in wastin' fine horseflesh on 'em."

The men who were guilty of the horrendous crime gaped at the sheriff with shock and disbelief, then hung their heads when he spat at their feet.

"Let's get movin'," said Sheriff Duffy, wheeling his horse around. He gazed at Silver Feather over his shoulder. "Good day!"

Silver Feather gave him a nod, then watched the men stumble behind the horses as they were led from the village.

"And now what of Harry Braddock?" Diana asked.

"I have plans for him," Silver Feather said tightly. "I will make the man pay for the desecration he has done—and not by the white man's law, by *mine.*"

"When do you plan to do this?" Diana asked, searching his eyes.

"For now, it is just good to have achieved what I have achieved," Silver Feather said.

He took her by the hand and led her back inside his cabin, then turned her to gaze into his eyes. "I have to make plans, careful and exact, about Harry Braddock," he said. "He will regret ever making a profit in this manner, for he will soon be brought face-to-face with the red man's kind of law."

Diana heard the determination and the bitterness in his voice.

She was seeing a new side to the man she loved. Yet she understood, for had he not had a lifetime of wrongs to make him bitter?

She was catapulted back to that day so long ago when he had been forced to witness the murder of his beloved parents.

"Whatever I can do to help, please tell me," she said quietly. "For you see, my love, your pain is my pain. All you need is to ask, and what you ask of me will be yours."

He drew her into his arms. "My Diana," he murmured against her lips. "My wonderful, sweet Diana."

Their lips met in a deep kiss, and Diana knew that no matter what happened to Silver Feather, he would never lose sight of what was right in this world of wrong.

Chapter 22

Let those love now who never loved before;
Let those who always loved,
Now love the more.

—Thomas Parnell

"Damn it all to hell," Harry Braddock raged as he paced back and forth in the library at Dettro Manor.

He swung around to face the young man who stood before him, wide-eyed and stiff. "Who played the main role in this?" he shouted. "Who is responsible for stopping the shipment?"

Earl Sharp shifted his feet nervously as he clasped his hands behind him. "The stagecoach driver had a big part in it," he said stiffly. "And, Harry, she ain't a man at all. She's female."

"I know what she is," Harry said, his voice filled with venom. "She's a traitor."

"You knew she was a lady?" Earl said, raising his eyebrows.

"Yeah, and I should've known she had an agenda," Harry said, waving his arms in the air.

He dropped his arms to his sides, doubling his

hands into tight fists as he glowered at Earl. "And she's in cahoots with Injuns, is she?"

"Seems so, but I'm not sure when they came together," Earl said. He smiled a slow, weaselly smile. "But I got the best of them all, Harry. They thought I was an innocent pup. I played my role so well that they actually let me go while they arrested the others."

"But why didn't they come for me?" Harry said, again pacing. He kneaded his chin thoughtfully.

"Maybe Diana—that's her name, you know— maybe Diana likes you," Earl said, his shoulders shaking as he chuckled darkly. "Maybe she's gonna come and marry you for your riches."

"Stop foolin' with me," Harry said, grabbing Earl by his collar. He halfway lifted him off the floor. "Don't make fun of ol' Harry. Do you hear?"

"I wasn't makin' fun of you," Earl choked out as he clawed at Harry's hand. "I was funnin' *with* you, not *at* you."

"This ain't no time for any kind of fun," Harry growled, stepping away from Earl. He went and stood before the fireplace, where a slow fire burned. "Why'n hell didn't they come for me after arrestin' the others?"

"All's I know is that I'm free as a bird and I'm hightailin' it outta here," Earl said, heading quickly for the door.

"Stop right there, you fool," Harry said, wheeling around and glaring at Earl. Earl stopped and slowly turned toward Harry, his head half ducked.

Harry grabbed Earl by the throat. "I want to hear it all from the beginning, do you understand?" he snarled. "I still don't have all of the pieces collected and put together."

"Let me go and I'll try to explain," Earl choked out. "Damn it, Harry, let me go or I won't tell you nothin'."

Harry hesitated, then dropped his hand. He pointed to a chair. "Sit," he commanded. "Then spill it all out again. I need to know what to expect now."

Earl scrambled to the overstuffed chair.

Harry sat opposite him. "Get it all out, Earl," he repeated. "I ain't got all day. They might even now be on their way to get me. I might just have to go into hidin'."

"Where'd you hide?" Earl asked, the knuckles of his fingers white as he clutched the arms of the chair.

"That's for me to know and you *not* to find out," Harry said.

He picked up a half-smoked cigar from an ashtray and stuck it between his teeth. He relit it, then settled back in the chair as he gazed intently at Earl.

He leaned closer to him. "Now, tell me again how this all came about so I can get it clear in my mind," he commanded for the third time.

"Your name was never mentioned around me," Earl said, sweat beading on his brow. He knew that Harry would just as soon shoot him as look at him, he had so little respect for another man's life.

"And again, why'd they let you go after arrestin' everyone else?" Harry said, taking the cigar from his mouth, resting it on the ashtray. He ran his fingers through his long, greasy hair.

"I had a good enough story that they believed," Earl said, chuckling. "I told 'em that I had a wife with child. I told 'em I only worked at this job because I couldn't find anything else anywheres else and that I needed to work to make money or my wife and child would suffer."

"That's a good one," Harry said, his eyes gleaming. "No woman'd have you."

"That's beside the point," Earl said, frowning. "They believed my lie. It saved me from the hoosegow. I'm free whilst those others are in jail."

"All right, you were smart at lyin'. So tell me the rest, from the beginnin'," Harry said, sighing with irritation. "Spit it out, Earl. Now."

"Oh, all right," Earl mumbled. "But only if after I'm through, you'll let me get outta here and put some miles between me and those damn Injuns. If'n they ever suspect I lied, they might scalp me and bury me so's only my head is exposed so that crawly creatures can finish me off. I've heard tell how savages treat their enemies."

"That ain't the way it happens," Harry said,

chuckling. "I mean, they don't bother buryin' a man now. They scalp 'em, then kill 'em, and then maybe they feed the corpse to their dogs."

"Damn it, Harry, that's enough of that kind of talk," Earl said, his voice trembling. "Do you want to hear what I've got to say or not? I'd rather just get up right now and leave, and never see your ugly face again."

"Go ahead. Tell me," Harry said, nodding.

"First let me say I was shocked all to hell when I discovered the trunks on my wagon were filled with rocks, not bones," Earl said dryly. "I was promised by the chief if I led him and his savages to the warehouse where the buttons were being made, he would let me go."

"You damn fool," Harry growled. "You are a tattler of the worst kind."

"I had no choice but to lead them there, or— or—I'd have been killed right then and there," Earl said.

"All right, just go on and tell me the rest," Harry grumbled. "Don't leave out one detail, do you hear?"

"The savages surrounded the place where the buttons and combs were being made and, like I said already, they took many captives, but they did let a few people go." Earl rushed through his account of what had happened.

"You say they let some of the people go?" Harry said, forking an eyebrow.

"Yep, some of the more innocent men and women were let go," Earl mumbled. "They mainly took the big shots captive."

"And then those captives were taken into custody by Sheriff Duffy of New Town," Harry said. He put his fingertips together before him as he became lost in thought.

Then he leaned toward Earl again. "And what's happened to Diana?" he asked guardedly. "Where is she now?"

"You'd better hold on to your hat when I tell you," Earl said, chuckling. "It just happens that she knew Chief Silver Feather many years ago, and now that they have found one another again, so to say, they are going to get married."

"Married?" Harry gasped, turning pale. "That pretty thing is marrying a redskin Injun?" He shuddered. "That disgusts me, absolutely disgusts me."

"I don't think you should be worryin' one iota about who she's marryin'," Earl said, rising. "I think your hide is what's at stake here. I don't trust those Injuns. I think they've let you stay free for some reason other than 'cause they like you."

"And what makes you think that?" Harry said, rising from the chair and walking beside Earl out of the room.

"It don't make no sense why they'd let you stay free after arrestin' the others," Earl said, opening the front door. He turned to Harry. "If I were you,

I'd hightail it outta here. Go where no one'll find you. You'll get off scot-free, for a while at least. Maybe you'll be forgotten and you can live a normal life again."

"No damn Injun is going to scare me into hiding," Harry said, walking out onto the wide front porch with Earl. He grabbed Earl by an arm. "Where is this Injun village? Maybe I need to pay them a surprise visit before they do it to me."

"You would risk goin' there?" Earl asked, walking down the steps, Harry still beside him. "You'll risk everything, Harry, if'n you go there and try to throw your weight around. You'd best let it rest. Maybe they aren't planning to do anything about you. They got the big shots at the other end. Surely that's all they need."

Harry grabbed Earl again. "I ain't letting a few savages scare me into early retirement. You know where the village is. Squat and draw me a map in the dirt so I can find my way to it."

"It ain't wise to do that," Earl said, yanking his arm free. "Leave it be, Harry. Right now you're free. Ain't that enough?"

"I'm free, but I still don't feel free. Those redskins might come in the dark of night and grab me from my bed," Harry mumbled. "Like I said, Earl. Draw me a map. Then you can tuck your tail between your legs and hightail it outta here. I don't need the likes of you hangin' 'round, causin' me trouble."

"You're trouble, not me," Earl said darkly. "I just get paid to deliver the bones. You actually do the stealin'. It ain't right stealin' from the dead. One day you'll be haunted by spirits that'll scare you right outta your pants."

"Hogwash," Harry spat out. He grabbed a stick and thrust it into Earl's hand. "Draw me that damn map, then get outta here. Do you hear? I don't like hearin' you talkin' that superstitious nonsense to me."

"It ain't superstitious nonsense," Earl said, taking the stick. "Injuns have ways we whites don't have. They can make magic happen, don't you know? They can breathe into the wind and suddenly there's an eagle flying. I just know I don't want any more association with them."

"Just draw me the damn map," Harry growled out. "Now, Earl. Not yesterday."

Earl drew what he remembered, which he knew was enough to get Harry where he wanted to go.

Then he stood, dropped the stick to the ground, and smiled. "All right, you've got your map, now how you gonna pay me for such valuable information?"

Harry's eyes gleamed. "How am I gonna pay you?" he said, laughing throatily.

He drew a pistol and aimed it at Earl. "This is how," he said, watching Earl take a shaky step away from him.

"You're gonna kill me?" Earl gulped out.

"Harry, damn it, you don't . . . have to . . . do that. I won't tell no one about you. Honest, Harry. Honest!"

"Beg, fool," Harry grumbled.

"Harry, you sonofabitch," Earl said. His eyes narrowed angrily. "I ain't beggin'. Just go ahead and kill me. My life ain't worth much anymore, anyhow."

"Aw, go on," Harry said, lowering his pistol to his side. "Get outta here."

Earl inched his way toward the hitching rail, then ran and mounted his steed. Without looking back, he sent his horse into a hard gallop.

Harry looked into the distance. His eyes squinted angrily as he thought of Diana being with Silver Feather. He gagged at the thought of her being in the Indian's arms.

He tucked his pistol back into its holster, then curled his fingers into tight fists when he envisioned Diana in bed with the redskin.

"It ain't gonna happen," he whispered to himself. "No. Injun, you ain't marryin' no white girl. I'm going to rescue Diana from the savages and take her as *my* bride."

Chapter 23

Love looks not with the eyes,
but with the mind, and, therefore,
is wing'd cupid painted blind.
　　　　　—William Shakespeare

Things had changed so quickly in Diana's life.

Today she wore the beautiful white doeskin dress and moccasins as she walked with the Choctaw women, learning how to gather herbs and roots. Silver Feather had said that he thought she might enjoy an outing with the women of his village while he took care of an urgent matter— making a decision about Harry Braddock and what his fate was to be.

She smiled as she thought back to this morning when she had awakened in Silver Feather's arms.

As Silver Feather ran his hands down her body, awakening it to even more sensual feelings that she had not known existed, he had said that it would not only be an invigorating day for her, even fun. It would be an opportunity for her, since he knew of her willingness to learn everything about the Choctaw. She was now a part of their lives—one with them, heart and soul.

He said the women would first collect herbs and dig roots. When they returned to the village, they would pick corn for the upcoming Green Corn Ceremony, an event that would introduce Diana into the culture of his people and the way they celebrated their success as growers of corn and gave thanks to the Great One Above, who had granted his blessings for the abundant crop.

Excited to learn everything about Silver Feather's people, especially since she was going to be the wife of their chief, Diana had eagerly agreed to his plan, though she hated being away from him for any length of time.

But she knew that she had to adjust to being away from him, for he was a chief with a chief's duties, which often did not include a woman's presence, not even a wife's.

She was suddenly aware of just how far the venture today had taken the women. It would take them at least an hour to get back to the village. Diana hoped that by the time they returned, Silver Feather would be through with his council.

She could hardly wait to share today's experiences with him and show him her basket of herbs and roots. She glanced at the sky and realized that by the time the women returned home, it would be dusk.

Although there was no reason to be concerned

about being this far from the village, since the women came this far all the time without their husbands, something was making Diana uneasy.

But she could not put her finger on just what it might be.

All the men who had been rounded up by Silver Feather and his warriors were surely behind bars now, awaiting their fate.

Then it came to her just why she was worried.

Two of the men associated with stealing the bones were still free, able to come and go as they pleased.

One was Earl Sharp, who was surely already reunited with his pregnant wife. The other was Harry Braddock, who might have received word about what had happened and could be on the warpath.

But surely he would not dare try to retaliate against a whole Choctaw clan. From what she had observed when she had been at Dettro Manor, she hadn't seen any people who might be employed by Harry Braddock. And being the sort of man that he was, he probably could not gather enough men who would dare to try it.

But it would make Diana's life much more comfortable if she knew that Braddock's fate had already been determined.

Pretty Fawn, a beautiful and newly married woman of Diana's age, came up beside her. "It was a good day for you?" she asked, her long braids bouncing against her back as she walked with Diana. She carried a basket of many roots and herbs, which would be used to season food. "Diana, do you believe you will remember which herbs are poisonous when we go again to gather them?"

"Yes, I truly believe I will be able to tell one from the other the next time we come to collect roots and herbs," Diana said, proudly lifting her chin, for she felt that she had had a successful learning experience today. "Thank you, Pretty Fawn, for taking so much time with me. I was afraid you might not get as many as you need since you were devoting so much time to pointing out things to me and teaching me how to dig the roots."

"I took what I needed, so do not be concerned about what I have or do not have for cooking meals for my new husband," Pretty Fawn said.

She suddenly looked bashfully down to her moccasined feet, then gazed at Diana again. "But in a few months I will be required to gather more than I did today. You see, I am with child," she said. "It is a miracle to be with child so soon after our wedding. My mother had warned me about hoping for a baby too soon, since it took her many moons to get with child herself."

"I'm so happy for you," Diana said, reaching out to touch Pretty Fawn's delicate-featured face gently. She then lowered her hand and gazed questioningly at Pretty Fawn. "How can you tell you are with child? My aunt was too shy to talk about such things to me, and my mother died when I was a little girl."

"Then I shall be your teacher," Pretty Fawn said, her face lighting up at the opportunity to be helpful once again to her chief's woman. "I shall tell you all that you need to know."

"That would be so kind of you," Diana said, realizing that she and Pretty Fawn had dropped back away from the others, so now they hurried their steps to catch up with them.

Pretty Fawn put one hand on her flat belly, the doeskin dress lying smooth against it. "We women have a time each month that is set aside for our bleeding, when we are kept separate from our men. I am sure white women bleed the same as we do." Her eyes were wide with wonder as she looked at Diana. "Is that so? Do you have a monthly flow, too?"

Seeing such innocence in Pretty Fawn's question, Diana smiled and nodded. "Yes, we have monthly flows, too. But it is not the custom of white women to live apart from the men, especially their husbands, during that time of the month. Will I have to be isolated from Silver Feather, too?"

"Yes, you must go into the menstrual hut with others who are there, until the bleeding stops," Pretty Fawn said. "It is taboo to be near all men, not only your husband, during your monthly flow."

Diana knew that there was an explanation for this, but she would ask about it later. She was eager to know about how a woman could tell that she was with child, for she hoped to have a baby soon after her marriage to Silver Feather. It would complete the miracle of their having found one another again.

"How do you know you are with child?" Diana prompted. "Silver Feather told me that you have been married for two months. Isn't it too soon to tell?"

"When a woman does not have her monthly flow the first time, she begins to hope that she is with child, but it is best to wait to tell anyone until the second flow does not come," Pretty Fawn said. "I have missed my second flow and soon will miss my third."

She giggled and her face flushed with color as she ducked her head, then looked up at Diana again. "My marriage is young, yet I am with child. My mother told me that the seed from my husband must have found its proper place inside my womb perhaps the very first night of our marriage."

"On the first night?" Diana said, her heart skipping a beat. "Actually . . . you believe you became with child the first time you shared lovemaking with your husband?"

"Perhaps, but it does not matter," Pretty Fawn said, smiling at Diana. "Having a child with my White Cloud will be a dream come true, for we both talked of children often while planning our marriage."

Diana only half heard what Pretty Fawn was saying, for she was recalling her first time with Silver Feather. It had been before vows had been spoken between them.

If she had gotten pregnant that first time she made love, the child would have been conceived without marriage vows!

She swallowed hard, for she remembered that her mother had spoken badly of women who became pregnant before they were married. She had called them loose women, and worse!

Diana did not want to label herself something so terrible. But she would not allow herself to feel any shame over having made love with Silver Feather. They had belonged to one another that first time, long ago, when they had met beside the lake, and they had belonged to one another since, even though they had been parted for so many years.

Suddenly her breath caught in her throat. She spied something on the hillside that reminded her of a promise that Silver Feather had made her so long ago. She couldn't believe her eyes as she stopped and gazed at the acres of bluebells.

She and the women had obviously taken a different way back to the village than the route they had followed when they ventured out that morning.

"Why do you stop?" Pretty Fawn asked. She stopped as well, looking from Diana to the bluebells and then back to Diana.

"I must have some," Diana said. She eyed her basket, glad that there was still some space in it. She was going to gather bluebells and take them back to show Silver Feather.

He knew how much she loved them, and why. They reminded her of her mother, who had loved these flowers so dearly, and of the promise Silver Feather had made so long ago.

"You must have flowers?" Pretty Fawn asked, raising an eyebrow. "They are lovely, but why are they so important to you?"

"Long ago, when I knew Silver Feather as a child, we gathered bluebells together," Diana answered. "He promised me bluebells on our wedding day."

"But we must hurry home," Pretty Fawn said as she glanced over her shoulder at the other women, who had kept walking toward the village without them.

"Go on without me," Diana said, already heading for the hill of flowers. "Please go on. I shall catch up with you soon."

"It is not wise that we get separated, even for a short while," Pretty Fawn said, again nervously

watching the other women, who seemed unaware
that Pretty Fawn and Diana had stopped. She
frowned at Diana. "We women have been taught
to stay together while away from our village. It is
safer that way."

"Then you go on and catch up with the others,"
Diana said again. She smiled at Pretty Fawn. "I'll
be all right. I won't be parted from you and the
others for very long. I only want a few flowers."

"I should stay and help, yet I feel my place is
with the others," Pretty Fawn said, again looking
nervously at the departing women. "I must go on,
Diana. Please hurry and catch up with us as fast as
you can."

"I shall," Diana said, running toward the hill,
the flowers drawing her to them like a moth to a
flame.

When she reached the flowers, she set her basket down, bent over, and ran her fingers through
the thickness of the delicate blue blossoms. "If
only Mama were here," she whispered to herself.

Suddenly caught up in painful feelings, Diana
sat down beside the flowers and burst into tears.
She had not known just how much she missed her
mother until now.

The pain in her heart was overwhelming. She
recalled the times when she would be out horseback riding and would come upon a patch of these
delicate blue flowers, and how she would eagerly
pick them and take them home to her mother.

She would never forget the happiness this small act brought her mother and how proudly she placed them in a vase of water and set them in the middle of the dining room table.

Oh, but those years were so far in the past.

She hadn't seen her mother for so long. Yet she felt her mother's presence all the time, in her heart.

She saw her mother's smile in her dreams. She heard her soft, sweet laughter in the wind.

Finding the flowers today brought her mother closer.

Drying her eyes, Diana got up and began plucking the flowers. She smiled inside, for she felt her mother smiling down at her from the heavens as she tucked a handful of bluebells into her basket.

"Just a few more," Diana whispered to herself. "Then I'll catch up with Pretty Fawn and the others."

Concentrating more on her upcoming marriage with Silver Feather rather than on the pangs of sadness and loneliness that came with thinking about her mother, Diana continued picking flowers until her basket was brimming with them.

"That should do it," she murmured, then turned to catch up with the others.

Her smile faded and panic rushed through her when she didn't see the women anywhere. Then she noticed a bend in the land, where trees blocked her view. She started to run.

Suddenly someone stepped out from the

bushes, his pistol drawn and aimed directly at Diana's belly, stopping her in midstep. Diana felt her heart plummet.

"You!" she gasped, dropping the basket. The flowers spilled out and scattered like blue rain at her feet.

Chapter 24

Is it, in Heav'n a crime,
to love too well?
To bear too tender or too
firm a heart?
— Alexander Pope

"Don't scream, or you'll die instantly," Harry Braddock snarled.

"You are the one looking death square in the eye for what you are doing, for you *will* die," Diana said, trying to show courage when in truth she was quaking with fear inside. "Silver Feather will see to that, you despicable, vile, disgusting snake. You're not even a man. You're a worm."

Harry's gaze roamed slowly over her, and he saw just how beautiful she was in a dress. He had never seen her in anything but men's breeches and shirts. Today her lovely, petite figure was well defined as the dress clung to her luscious curves.

Then something else came to him that made him want to vomit. Earl Sharp had said that Diana was going to marry Chief Silver Feather. The mere thought of such a thing as that was disgusting.

His eyes narrowed angrily. "You had to interfere, didn't you, and side with Injuns instead of people of your own skin color," he said between clenched teeth.

He shivered at the thought of her having already cavorted with the redskin, something that was taboo in the white world.

Yet he hungered for what lay beneath the dress, despite the possibility that a redskin might already have touched her.

He knew that he must get her away from there before the squaws missed her and came looking for her. He didn't want to have to kill any of the squaws, for he knew that would bring the whole world of Choctaw Indians down hard on him.

Yet surely one missing lady wouldn't cause such a commotion. No one was a witness to what he was doing, and no one knew what he planned to do with Diana. They would have no reason to suspect it was him.

"Come with me," Harry said, motioning with his pistol toward the thick cover of trees, only a few feet from the lovely hill of bluebells. "Now! Do you hear? I've got plans for you that don't include anyone else."

He leaned into her face. "You're too pretty to kill, but I wouldn't blink an eye if I was forced into killin' any squaw who might come lookin' for you. Ever since I realized you were a woman, I've wanted you, and by damn, now I have you. I'm taking you home."

"I won't be there for long," Diana said, wincing when he grabbed her roughly by an arm and yanked her into the shadow of the trees, where a horse was tethered. "Silver Feather will come for me."

"Like I said, Silver Feather won't even know where you are," Harry snarled, shoving her toward the horse. "And if he does come to my house looking for you, you'll be well hidden. I'll keep you in hiding until Silver Feather gives up looking for you."

He leaned into her face. "If it means keepin' you in hidin' for months, it'll be worth it—or should I say, *you'll* be worth it," he said, his eyes gleaming.

Truly afraid for herself and any women who might come looking for her, Diana looked past Harry, but no one was in sight.

For the moment, she had no choice but to do what Harry told her to do. She hoped to find a way to outwit him and soon regain her freedom.

"Get on my horse and don't try anything, or I'll shoot you," Harry snarled.

Diana swung herself into the saddle and closed her eyes as he mounted behind her, then snaked an arm around her waist and pulled her back against his body. She realized that he still held the gun, in the same hand as the reins, which made it impossible for her to try to escape.

She knew that he would kill her to silence her— she was only a roll in the hay to him, so to speak.

He could get the same from any woman who roamed the back streets and alleys of New Town.

"Just remember what I said," Harry growled as he rode away with her toward the plantation where she had grown up. "You ain't nothin' to me. Nothin'. I'll kill you if I get even a hint of you tryin' somethin' that might draw attention to us."

"I won't," Diana murmured, tears burning at the corners of her eyes.

This morning everything in her life had been sweet and wonderful. But now that was just a memory, and it might never be anything but a memory, for this man seemed intent on having her.

If he had gone to all this trouble to find her, she doubted that he would allow anything to stand in the way of his having her all to himself.

But then it came to her. How had he known where she was, and with whom?

Earl? she wondered to herself.

Had Earl not been truthful with her and Silver Feather? Had he actually been in on all of this with Harry? In time, surely she would know the answer to that question. But for now she had to focus on survival—hers.

Suddenly Diana remembered the bluebells. She had dropped the basket when Harry had come upon her so suddenly.

That basket of flowers and the other things that she had gathered now lay on the ground. Perhaps it would reveal what had happened to her—that she had been abducted.

She knew that the one who would be looking for her would be Silver Feather. He would follow the trail of this man's horse hoofprints, for weren't all Indians good at tracking?

Especially someone as astute as Silver Feather?

Yes, she did hold out some hope of being rescued.

"I can just see that mind of yours working," Harry said, laughing raucously as Dettro Manor came into sight. Harry apparently knew a shortcut that took them there much more quickly than the usual route. "Just relax, Diana. You ain't goin' anywheres for a while, except into hidin'."

"And where do you think you can hide me well enough to keep Silver Feather from finding me should he come looking?" Diana asked, her voice drawn.

"First of all, there ain't no way in hell that Silver Feather can figure out who grabbed you," Harry said. "That means wherever I take you will be good enough."

"There isn't anyplace that you can hide me that will keep Silver Feather away from me," Diana snapped at him. "Now that he and I have found each other again, there will be hell to pay for the one who stands in our way, and that is you, Harry. You."

"We'll see about that," he said, riding on up to Dettro Manor.

He dismounted, then pulled her off the horse and gave her a shove toward the house. "I'm locking you in the attic until I feel it's safe to let you out again," he said, now half dragging her up the front steps. "Then I'll get me a preacher and we'll be married. You'll be the belle of the manor. I'll call this place Braddock Hall. Now ain't that nice? Braddock Hall. Yep, I like it. Just think about it, Diana. You're home."

"This hasn't been a home for many years now," Diana said, almost tripping when they reached the porch.

He grabbed her and steadied her.

"When you become my wife, you'll turn this place into a home again, especially when you bring children into the world for me," he said, taking her inside.

She stopped, turned, and spat at his feet.

"Never," she screamed. "Never!"

"You'll change your mind after you're cooped up alone in the attic for a while," Harry said, leading her by an elbow up the stairs. "And I must keep you there for quite a spell to make certain that Silver Feather can't get even a scent of you. After a while, he'll forget you. That's when I'll see that our nuptials are carried out."

Again she stopped and spat at his feet.

"All right, then, be stubborn," he said, shrugging. "In time you will act different."

He led her on up to the attic, shoved her inside, then locked the door behind her.

A slow, smug smile fluttered across Diana's lips, for she knew something that Harry Braddock surely didn't know, or he wouldn't have left her there.

But she must wait until dark before making her way through the secret passageways. She would, by damn, be with Silver Feather in time to celebrate the Green Corn Ceremony with him and his people!

Chapter 25

Ring out the want, the care, the sin,
The faithless coldness of the time.
                        —Alfred Lord Tennyson

"Chief! Chief!"

Pretty Fawn shouted for him in a desperate, frightened tone. Silver Feather rushed from the council house just as she reached the door, breathing hard, one hand hanging on to a basket filled with herbs and roots.

"What is it, Pretty Fawn?" he asked, looking past her to the rest of the women, standing in a cluster, their eyes wide with silent fear.

"It is—it is—" Pretty Fawn stammered, finding it hard to say the words that she knew would concern, then anger, her chief.

"It is what?" Silver Feather said, placing his hands on her slender shoulders. "What are you finding so hard to say, and—and where is Diana?"

"I cannot say where she is," Pretty Fawn said, tears suddenly in her eyes. "My chief, she stayed behind as we women came back to our village.

But—but I expected her to catch up with us. She said that she would."

"What do you mean, she stayed behind?" Silver Feather said tightly, dropping his hands from Pretty Fawn's shoulders. "Why?"

"As we were on our way home after a fruitful day of gathering herbs and roots, Diana saw—" She stopped again. She knew that should she continue speaking she would upset her chief even more than she already had.

Diana was gone!

"Go on, Pretty Fawn," Silver Feather said, his patience running thin. "If you do not hurry and tell me, I will go to the other women. Surely they are more courageous than you."

"Your woman—your future bride—saw flowers that drew her to them," Pretty Fawn finished quickly.

"Flowers?" Silver Feather said, raising an eyebrow. "What flowers?"

"The blue flowers on the hillside. Bluebells," Pretty Fawn said, finally able to talk without stammering and looking foolish in her chief's eyes. "Diana wanted to gather a bouquet."

"And did she?" Silver Feather said, searching Pretty Fawn's midnight-black eyes.

"When I left her she had not yet begun, but she had set her basket down so that she could," Pretty Fawn said.

"You left her there alone, even though you

women are taught to stay together?" Silver Feather said, his eyes narrowing angrily.

"The others had already walked far ahead of us because Diana and I were talking to one another," Pretty Fawn said softly. "I like her so much. It was such a pleasure to have her at my side today. She was so eager to learn our customs."

"Did you teach her that it is never wise to stray from the others?" Silver Feather asked, his fists on his hips. He glowered at her. "And if she is not with you, does that mean that she is still gathering flowers? Did you go back for her and she still refused to come with you and the others?"

"When she did not catch up with us, yes, the others and I went back to get her," Pretty Fawn said, her voice breaking.

"If you went back for Diana, where is she?" Silver Feather asked, his pulse racing, for he already knew what her answer would be.

"She was gone," Pretty Fawn gulped out. She lowered her eyes. "I am the guilty one, for I should have never agreed to let her stay behind. If anything happens to her—"

Silver Feather had heard enough. "Direct me to the place where you last saw my Diana," he said, taking the basket from Pretty Fawn and setting it on the ground. "You are good at riding horses. Go now. Get your steed. You will ride with me."

Pretty Fawn's eyes widened. "You want me to ride with you?" she asked, honored by his suggestion, yet still feeling guilty for what had happened to Diana.

"Go," Silver Feather said flatly. "Explain to your husband where you are going. He will understand."

Pretty Fawn slid her hand over her belly. Would riding a horse harm her unborn child? Most women did not ride a horse once they knew they were with child.

But she could not disappoint her chief by begging off going with him. She felt responsible for what happened to Diana.

She nodded to Silver Feather, then went to her husband, who had just stepped out of the council house to find out what was transpiring between his wife and his chief. Her voice had carried to him.

"I must go with our chief," she said, gazing into the eyes that always mesmerized her. "White Cloud, I feel that it is my fault that Diana is missing."

"I heard part of what was being said between you and our chief, that his woman did not return with you and the other women. He wants you to lead him to where his woman was last seen," White Cloud answered.

He took her hands in his as he looked past her and saw Silver Feather walking to the corral to get his horse.

Then White Cloud looked into his woman's

eyes again. "I shall join you and our chief in the hunt."

Pretty Fawn flung herself into his arms. "I am so happy that you are not ashamed of me for having let our chief down," she sobbed. "What if something bad has happened to Diana?"

"This is not the time to think of such a thing," White Cloud said. He gently placed his hands on her shoulders. He looked intently into her eyes. "Go for your horse as I go for mine."

Pretty Fawn nodded, then ran to the corral with her husband.

They were soon in their saddles and riding alongside Silver Feather back in the direction whence Pretty Fawn had just come.

Every horse's hoofbeat on the solid ground felt like claps of thunder inside Pretty Fawn's head.

And the farther they traveled, the more afraid she became that something terrible might have happened to Diana.

She glanced down at her stomach, and noticed how her body was jolted by each gallop of the horse. She prayed to the Great One Above that he would keep her child safe and would deliver them all to Diana wherever she might be, hopefully unharmed.

Silver Feather was lost in his own thoughts as he rode hard in the direction that Pretty Fawn had pointed out to him.

He recalled outings with Diana when they were

young and always eager to go horseback riding whenever she could sneak one of her stepfather's horses from the stable.

How often had they gone past that hillside some distance from Dettro Manor, where the ground had been covered with bluebells? How often had they stopped and gathered bluebells together for her mother, even though taking them home would be a confession of her horseback riding?

But when her mother had questioned her about being on the horse, riding away from the turmoil of Dettro Manor, Diana had never openly confessed that she had been with Silver Feather. Of course, he suspected her mother knew the truth but chose not to interfere. Silver Feather believed she understood the restlessness of her daughter and never attempted to quell it.

It seemed only natural for Diana to stop if she came across a hillside covered with bluebells.

"We are almost there," Pretty Fawn shouted over to Silver Feather. "Just around that bend."

Silver Feather sank his moccasined heels into the flanks of his steed and rode hard away from Pretty Fawn and White Cloud.

When he reached the hillside of bluebells and saw no signs of Diana anywhere, his heart sank. He rode alongside the flowers, intent on finding some evidence of Diana. He did not hear when

Pretty Fawn and White Cloud arrived and drew a tight rein a few feet from him.

All that Silver Feather could think about was his Diana and where she might have disappeared to.

He was certain that she would not have gone away on her own. Someone had to have come along and forced her to go with them.

His eyes searched for crushed grass, which was as helpful as tracks in dirt when trying to find someone. He rode slowly onward. He felt as if his heart stopped dead inside his chest when he saw the basket on the ground a few feet ahead of him. The spilled flowers and herbs were evidence that Diana had been there.

He quickly dismounted. He touched the spilled bluebells gingerly, his heart thudding like drums being beaten inside his chest.

He looked around, searching for any clue that might help him solve this puzzle of his missing woman.

Pretty Fawn came to him on foot. "I did not see the basket when I came back for her. I did not walk this far around the hill."

She stifled a sob, then ran back to her husband. She flung herself into White Cloud's arms as he stood beside his steed, watching the grief pass over the face of his chief.

Suddenly Pretty Fawn's eyes widened. She grabbed her belly when she felt something warm between her thighs.

"What is it?" White Cloud asked, his gaze locking on what he knew was blood spotting her doeskin dress. "No, Pretty Fawn. Do not tell me—"

"Our child," she sobbed, then fainted in her husband's arms.

Having seen what was happening and the blood on Pretty Fawn's dress, Silver Feather ran to White Cloud and gazed sadly at his friend's lovely wife. Silver Feather heard what she had said about a child, and he was filled with regret.

He shook his head back and forth. "Had I known of your wife's delicate condition, I would not have asked her to come with me," he said. "Now whoever is responsible for my wife's disappearance is responsible for what has happened to your wife as well."

He placed an arm around White Cloud's shoulder. "Return home with your wife," he said, his voice breaking. "Let our shaman care for Pretty Fawn. Perhaps the child is still safe inside her womb and her riding the horse caused the bleeding, but nothing else."

He stepped away from them. "Go. I shall say a prayer for you and the child as I pray for my woman," he said.

"Chief, do you want me to send warriors to help in your search?" White Cloud asked as he gently carried his wife to his steed.

Silver Feather was deep in thought as he weighed his options. When he thought about

Diana's apparent abduction, only one man came to mind.

Harry Braddock!

If Harry Braddock had somehow found out that Silver Feather was responsible for his having lost money, would he try to find a way to make Silver Feather pay?

"I will go on alone," Silver Feather answered. "Go and care for your woman and the child. I will care for my own woman. I will find her, and whoever stole her away will pay in the worst way."

"Do you know who did this?" White Cloud asked as he gently handed Pretty Fawn to Silver Feather to hold while White Cloud mounted his horse.

"There is only one man who comes to mind," Silver Feather said, now handing Pretty Fawn up to White Cloud, who carefully positioned her on his lap, so that her head rested against his chest.

White Cloud slid a protective arm around her waist and took up his horse's reins with his other hand.

"I feel it is best that I work alone right now," Silver Feather said. "But after I get Diana back home with me, I will bring you and my other warriors in on my act of vengeance."

"How can you be so certain of who did this?" White Cloud asked as he turned his steed back toward the village.

"Just know that I am," Silver Feather said, running to his horse and mounting it in one leap.

He nodded to White Cloud and Pretty Fawn, then rode off at a hard gallop toward Dettro Manor.

"Diana, I am coming for you," he shouted into the wind. "I will save you. Pity the man who did this to you!"

Chapter 26

*Heard, have you? What? They have
told you he never repented his sin.*
— Alfred Lord Tennyson

As a faint light poured through a tiny round window on the wall at the top of the attic, tears streamed from Diana's eyes. She looked slowly around her at all the familiar things.

It was apparent that Harry Braddock had not taken the time to discard her family's possessions but instead had simply brought everything up to the attic and left it there.

Diana immediately recognized a trunk that had been brought from her stepfather's bedroom, where it had rested at the foot of his bed.

She had always thought that he had left it there as a way to keep her mother close to him after she died, for her mother's personal belongings had been stored in it.

Diana gazed anxiously at the tapestry that hung on the far wall, knowing that freedom lay behind it, for behind it was the access to passageways that led from the house, out past where the cotton fields had once been. But she felt that she should wait until later tonight to escape, when Harry would more than likely be asleep. Before his bedtime he might come and take a greedy look at her, or worse.

Now she had to pass the time until she felt it was safe to make her escape. There was no better way to do this than to go through her mother's things.

Ever since she had found the hillside of bluebells, she had not been able to get her mother and how much she missed her off her mind. It had been many years since her death, but because of their closeness, those years without her had sometimes been pure agony.

But now that Diana had found Silver Feather, he would help mend that broken part of her heart that had come with the death of her mother.

Diana knelt before the trunk. Slowly she raised the lid. The air was suddenly filled with the perfume of her mother.

It was on the silk dresses that were folded neatly in place. It was on the lacy handkerchiefs.

"Mama," she sobbed as she held a dress endearingly in her arms, against her chest. She buried her nose in it.

Her past flowed through her mind: sitting on her mother's lap, hearing her mother's voice telling her stories and singing softly to her until Diana had fallen into a sweet slumber.

Then Diana saw something else. It was her mother's diary!

Diana's eyes misted with tears when she recalled having many times watched her mother sit at her personal desk, entering passages in this very same diary.

Her mother would be dressed in her silk finery, her golden hair tied in a bun atop her head, her delicate fingers holding down one side of the diary as she wrote on the opposite page.

Her mother had never offered the diary to Diana for reading, and Diana had never taken it upon herself to read it. She had always thought that would be too intrusive.

But now it was different. Her mother was gone. Only her memories remained. And the diary would surely awaken even more precious memories.

She placed the dress gently on the oak floor beside her and lifted the diary from the trunk. Her fingers trembled as she opened the bound book that had her mother's initials engraved in gold on the pale lilac velveteen cover.

There was just enough light wafting through the small window overhead for her to be able to make out her mother's handwriting. Her mother had had such exquisite penmanship.

Diana smiled through her tears as she began

reading, discovering so much about her mother that she had not known before. She was unaware that her mother had loved her second husband so much and that she had looked past his greedy ways and his need to enslave Indians.

Otherwise, her mother had written, her second husband had been a good man whose intentions were pure toward most people.

Diana read about how her mother was so happy that Jamieson had treated Diana as his own child since her mother could not have any more children because of a mishap when she had given birth to Diana.

Her mother had found one thing, though, about her second husband's behavior toward Diana that troubled her. He had taught her too many things that he would have taught a son.

Her mother had abhorred Diana's taking target practice with Jamieson, and then again Diana's quickly learning the art of riding horses.

"Mama, it is good that my stepfather taught me those things. If he hadn't, perhaps I would be married to someone I didn't love out of the need to have food and shelter. Or I might be dead."

As it was, Diana had been able to fend very well for herself until she found the man she truly wanted to make a life with.

Diana turned the pages and continued reading.

She read some passages more slowly, tears filling her eyes.

Her mother had written of Diana and Diana's feelings for Silver Feather. Her mother had found it sweet.

She had written that she would never tell her husband about the deep feelings that Diana had for Silver Feather. It was already apparent to her that her husband resented the young Indian brave, and especially his Choctaw family.

The diary was thick, so Diana skimmed through it quickly. She would start from the very beginning again, later, to read it more slowly and absorb those special entries that warmed her heart.

Diana was startled when she read her mother's descriptions of the pains in her heart—afraid that death might be near—

That was where the diary ended.

Apparently her mother had died shortly thereafter.

"Mama, oh, Mama," she moaned, tears streaming from her eyes.

Sighing, she set the diary next to the dress on the floor, then began pushing other pieces of clothing aside inside the trunk.

Soon something caught her eye. There was a box at the bottom of the trunk.

"Why is this here?" Diana whispered to herself, lifting the heavy box out.

The box did seem purposely hidden there. But by whom? Harry Braddock?

Or her stepfather before he had died?

It made more sense that her stepfather would have placed it there, for why would Harry bother to hide it beneath her mother's finery?

Diana thought back to those days when she was trying to find the papers that would free the Choctaw. She had gone through this trunk. She had found nothing there except her mother's things.

But now?

Opening the box, Diana recognized several of her stepfather's journals, private and otherwise. Then she saw several rolled-up papers, the strings that tied them looking yellowed and ancient.

Her heart began thumping wildly within her chest.

If this was what she thought it might be, finally she had found what she had wanted to find for Silver Feather so long ago.

Oh, yes, surely these items were placed in the trunk by her stepfather, then brought to the attic by Harry Braddock along with everything else that he didn't bother to throw away.

Trembling with anticipation and hope, Diana dumped the box out onto the floor. She set the journals aside, then untied the strings from the rolled-up papers, and one by one, unrolled and read them.

Her heart seemed to stop when she realized that these were indeed the very papers that she had searched for those long years ago. Her eyes hurried over the words, and she slowly smiled.

She read how her stepfather had cleverly duped the Choctaw by laying out contracts that had been forged to make the Choctaw believe they had signed away their land to the landowner.

It had always been theirs. And it still was.

Hardly able to contain her excitement, Diana folded the most important paper to hide it as she took it from the attic to Silver Feather. Smiling broadly she tucked the folded paper inside the bodice of her dress.

She focused on the tapestry on the wall.

She was eager to flee and hurry to Silver Feather to hand over the paper that could change his life.

But she had to be patient. It was still daylight.

She had to wait until she was certain Harry Braddock was asleep.

But the waiting would be grueling!

She scrambled around, putting everything back inside the trunk and closing it—and just in time. She leaped to her feet and went to sit across the room, far from the trunk, just as Harry Braddock entered with a tray of food.

"Thought I'd forgot you, didn'tcha?" he said, laughing throatily.

"No, I knew better than that," Diana said dryly.

"I've brought you somethin' to eat," he said. "And then I'll leave you be. I'm too tuckered out to take you into my bed tonight for some fun. But to-morrow?"

He chuckled and leaned his face down closer to hers. "Yep, tomorrow I'll show you just how this ol' boy knows how to please a lady," he said huskily, his eyes gleaming.

Diana glared at him but didn't say anything, for she knew that he would have a surprise tomorrow when he came for her. She would be long gone.

And so would the paper that would return everything to the Choctaw.

Chapter 27

O! He give to us his joy,
That our grief he may destroy,
Till our grief is fled and gone.
                    —William Blake

After sitting in the dark for what seemed long enough to have finally reached the midnight hour and truly believing it was safe for her to attempt her escape, Diana took a last, lingering look at the trunk, where so many memories of her past were stored.

She knew that there was the possibility that she would never get the chance to see and touch her mother's things again. But if everything worked out she would be back. She would share those things with Silver Feather.

"I must hurry," she whispered to herself, lifting the tapestry that led to her freedom.

The important paper still tucked safely against her bosom, Diana stepped into a blackness such as she had never seen before. Always before, when she had been in the passageways, she had carried a lantern or lamp. But tonight she had neither.

Harry Braddock had not been civil enough to leave a lamp in the attic for her, but thankfully the moon had provided enough light—until now.

When Diana started moving slowly down the passageway, having memorized its every curve and turn those long years ago, she stretched her hands out before her.

She shuddered when one hand swept through thick cobwebs, hoping that no hideous spider would be there. She could hear the squeaking of rats everywhere, and even felt one rushing across one of her feet.

Trying not to think about rats and spiders being there with her in the passageway, she kept going onward.

She found more and more cobwebs, which proved that no one had been in the passageway since she had been there with Silver Feather those long years ago. Surely that meant that Harry Braddock had no idea that these passageways existed.

Diana felt confident that she would soon find freedom at the end of the passageway. She had always come out just past the rich cotton fields—where nothing grew now but weeds.

Her heart pounding with anticipation, she hurried onward, remembering this turn and that, knowing which would take her back to the house in various places and which would lead her outside.

Finally she saw moonlight at the far end. She was almost there.

Her only fear was that she might have been fooling herself into believing that Harry Braddock knew nothing of the passageways. He could be standing at the end this very minute, waiting for her.

She breathed a sigh of relief when she stepped out into the moonlight and found nothing but fresh air—and freedom!

She inhaled the sweetness of the breeze, savoring it since the air inside the passageway had been so thick with the repugnant smells of damp and mildew.

She gazed heavenward. "Thank you, Lord," she breathed, grateful that she had been able to escape.

She looked over her shoulder, back in the direction of the corral, where she knew at least one horse was there for the taking.

But she was afraid to get that close to the house. Harry might hear the horse when she took it.

No. She could not risk it.

She had to hope that she could find help at a house somewhere close by.

Diana rushed into the darkness of the trees, then began running.

She ran until her side ached unmercifully. Yet even with her heart pounding, her breath coming in short rasps, she continued on.

She hoped to find a safe place. She wasn't sure

how much farther she could go at her current pace. Her knees were strangely rubbery from exhaustion, and her mouth was dry.

Panting, with sweat running from her brow even though it was a cool evening, Diana stopped to rest for a moment. She leaned back against a tree and buried her face in her hands.

Then her heart skipped a beat. She raised her face quickly and stiffened when she heard a horse approaching out of a copse.

What if it's Harry? she thought to herself, a sharp pang of fear stabbing at her gut.

Afraid to move, Diana stood stiffly against the tree, peering through the trees to see who was there. The horse was only a few feet away now.

She realized only now that night had turned to dawn. She had been concentrating so hard on getting as far as she could from Dettro Manor that she had not even noticed that it was no longer dark!

Surely whoever was near would see her. She desperately sought someplace else to hide.

When she saw a stand of thick bushes only a few footsteps away, she hurried behind them. Parting a few branches, she watched as the horse and rider came into full view.

She could hardly believe her eyes!

It was Silver Feather!

"Lord, thank you, thank you," she cried as she hurried from behind the bushes and stepped out in front of Silver Feather.

When he saw Diana standing there, he thought for a moment that it might be an apparition, but the closer he got to her, the more he was sure that it was Diana in the flesh.

"Silver Feather!" Diana cried as he came up to her and drew a tight rein.

He dismounted and grabbed her into his arms. They clung. She cried. He marveled at having found her.

They embraced a few moments longer, then he held her away from him and gazed into her eyes. "Tell me what happened and who is responsible," he said grimly. "When Pretty Fawn came to me and told me that you were gone, I feared that I would never see you again. I went and found your basket. I knew that someone had abducted you. Who did this, Diana? Who?"

"Harry Braddock," she answered, wiping tears from her face. "He was actually planning to force me into marrying him."

"He is a man who will regret crossing me," Silver Feather growled.

"What are you going to do?" Diana asked, searching his eyes. "I want a role in his comeuppance. I want to help with whatever you have planned."

"Soon you will see what my plan is," Silver Feather said, taking her hands in his. "I'm just glad that you are with me again."

His eyes wavered. "Did he—touch—you?" he asked thickly. "Did he force himself—?"

She slid a hand free and placed it gently against his lips, stopping him from saying what she knew was on his mind.

"No, he didn't defile my body," she murmured. "But had I been in the attic when he went for me this morning, he would have. He told me as much."

Suddenly she remembered what was tucked beneath the bodice of her dress, the touch of the paper cool against her breasts.

Her eyes widened with excitement as she reached inside and took out the folded paper.

"Here," she said, holding it out for him. "This is yours."

He took it, and as he unfolded it, he gazed at Diana questioningly. "What is it?"

"Do you remember that long years ago I searched for the papers that proved my stepfather cheated your Eagle Clan out of your land?" she asked, smiling broadly at him.

"Yes. How could I forget?" he said, then his eyes widened as he realized what she was trying to say.

"This paper proves your claim, Silver Feather," Diana said excitedly. "Read it. You shall see. I am so happy for you, Silver Feather, for all the land where Dettro Manor and the cotton fields sit, is yours—is your Choctaw people's. It is written in black and white. My stepfather showed your father false papers that he forged to fool him. But these are the proper ones."

As he read, Diana watched him, then smiled at him when he gazed at her, beaming with happiness.

"And so now you see how my stepfather duped your people," she said. "Inch by inch, they had their land stolen from them, as well as their dignity."

Suddenly she heard more horses and saw that the riders were Silver Feather's warriors.

"I rode on ahead of my warriors because I had planned to go into the passageways at Dettro Manor and see if you were there," Silver Feather told Diana. "I told my warriors to wait, then to come to Dettro Manor and surround it. I could not help but believe that was where I would find you."

"And you were right," Diana said, then told him how everything had happened. "And so you see, you were right to suspect Harry Braddock."

"You said that he locked you in the attic," Silver Feather said, glancing over his shoulder in the direction of Dettro Manor. "He might have already discovered that you are gone."

"He apparently doesn't know about the passageways," Diana replied. She laughed throatily. "I would have liked to see the look on his face when he discovered that I was gone yet the lock on the door had not been disturbed."

Diana frowned. "We must hurry to the manor.

Once he does discover that I'm gone, he might try
to flee."

Silver Feather turned to his warriors, who had
drawn a tight rein behind him. "We must hurry on
to Dettro Manor!" he shouted. "We might already
be too late to capture the evil man!"

They all nodded.

Silver Feather folded the paper and handed it
back to Diana. "Please keep this in a safe place
while we go and stop Harry Braddock," he said.

Smiling, Diana took the paper and slid it back
inside her bodice.

Silver Feather reached down and swept Diana
onto his horse with him, positioning her behind
him in the saddle. She clung to his waist as he
snapped his reins and rode at a hard gallop toward
Dettro Manor, the others dutifully following.

When Dettro Manor finally came into view, Silver Feather raised a hand as a signal for his men to
stop.

"Quietly, but quickly, surround the estate
grounds," he ordered. "Diana and I know a secret
passage that will take us inside the house. If you
see Harry Braddock trying to flee, stop him."

He described the man to them.

Then he wheeled his horse around and rode
back to where the passageway began, at the edge
of what had been the cotton field.

He tethered his steed to a low limb, then
grabbed his rifle from the gunboot and took a pis-

tol from his travel bag and slapped it into Diana's hand. Together they dashed into the darkness of the passageway.

They ran along it until they came to the place where the passageway led to one of the upstairs bedrooms.

Diana pushed on the wall to open a panel inside the room.

"We must be careful as we step into the room," she whispered to Silver Feather.

They passed through the opening together, and she quickly closed it.

"I have no idea where he might be," she murmured. "If he hasn't risen yet, he might still be in his room. Let's go and see."

Diana led Silver Feather into the corridor, but they hurried back inside the room and closed the door when they heard someone running down the stairs that led from the attic.

"It must be Harry," Diana whispered to Silver Feather. "No one else lives in this house. As far as I know, he doesn't even have a maid. That means he has surely found me gone. We must stop him."

They waited until they heard him right outside the room where they were hiding. Then, as Diana held the pistol steady, Silver Feather readied the rifle for firing. They opened the door and stepped out right into Harry Braddock's path. He stared disbelievingly from one to the other, a pistol in his right hand.

"You? How did you get out of the attic? And how did you get into my house?" Harry looked from Diana to Silver Feather. He backed slowly away from them. He felt trapped, for he knew that he couldn't shoot them both at the same time. Whoever he left alive would kill him before he could fire again.

"Your house?" Silver Feather said, holding his rifle steady on the man's gut. "This has never been your house, nor was it Colonel Jamieson Dettro's." He nodded at Diana. "Show him the papers."

Smiling smugly, she took the paper from inside her dress, unfolded it, and read what was written on it.

She saw the confusion on Harry's face.

Then he laughed. "It doesn't matter none," he said mockingly. "This place never meant anything to me except as a place where I could deal in bones."

His eyes narrowed sharply as he looked at Silver Feather. "But now you've gone and spoiled even that for me," he snarled. His gaze moved to Diana. "And how in the hell did you escape from the attic? I couldn't believe my eyes. The lock was still in place!"

"Do you think I would really tell you?" Diana said.

"Naw, nothin' matters now, anyway," Harry grumbled. "Seems you got me. What are you going to do with me?"

"Although I would like nothing more than to take care of you myself, I wouldn't want the white man's law breathing down my neck," Silver Feather said. "I plan to take you to New Town. I'll let the sheriff decide your fate. It will be enough for me that you will no longer be able to do evil things against my people."

"Sheriff Chance Duffy?" Harry said, paling. He took an unsteady step away from Silver Feather and Diana. He looked down and away, then back up with an angry glint in his eye. He lunged toward Silver Feather, tripping over a braided rug while doing so.

He got his feet tangled, then started falling, but before he reached the floor, he grabbed the barrel of Silver Feather's rifle and it discharged.

Diana gasped with alarm when she saw Harry clutch at his chest. Blood seeped between his fingers.

Harry gasped and fell to his knees, his eyes still on Diana.

"You—" he got out, then crumpled to the floor, his eyes locked in a death stare.

A shiver raced up and down Diana's spine. She turned and embraced Silver Feather.

"It's all over," she whispered.

She leaned away from him. "I will go into New Town, tomorrow, to the courthouse to clear up the confusion about the house and grounds," she said, her voice gaining strength. "I will ask if someone might know something about your Eagle Clan, what might have happened to them."

She glanced over at Harry. "I'll also see that someone comes for him, and I'll explain how he died."

She took Silver Feather's hand. "Let's get out of here," she said, walking beside him through the house and outside. He waved his men down to the house.

"My warriors, I have good news," he said, pride in his voice as he told them about the paper and what it disclosed.

Diana glanced back at the house. She was so glad that the house belonged to someone worthy of it and that she could still have her mother's belongings, to keep with her forever.

She looked up at Silver Feather as he talked to his warriors, with such pride in his stance and joy in his eyes. Finally, after so many years of injustice, things were on their way to being righted.

Chapter 28

Do! I tell you, I rather guess,
She was a wonder, and nothing less!
—Oliver Wendell Holmes

The flames of a great fire leaped high into the sky, and around it the Choctaw people gathered.

Silver Feather was with the men, while Diana sat with the women. She was proud that she had been able to do something special for Silver Feather. She had actually found what remained of Silver Feather's lost Eagle Clan.

They were all there now around the sacred fire, mingling with the Turtle Clan. It was the night before the great Green Corn Ceremony, when several smaller ceremonies, involving imagery similar to that of the Green Corn Ceremony were performed, serving to solidify the Choctaw relationship with ABA, the sanctity of their sacred circle, and their sense of common identity and history.

While the women sat in a wide circle around the huge sacred fire, singing, the men stood in an outer circle behind them, singing in musical ca-

dence with their *ohichicouas*, gourd rattles filled
with small pebbles.

Although Diana was attempting to learn these
songs tonight, she could not stop thinking about
what she had achieved yesterday. It had all happened when she had gone into New Town with the
paper that proved that Silver Feather and his people were the true owners of Dettro Manor and the
land that surrounded it.

After finalizing the paperwork for Silver
Feather, ensuring that no one would ever dupe
him or his people again, she had asked a few government officials about the Eagle Clan. She
queried whether or not anyone knew where they
might have gone after Colonel Jamieson Dettro
had died. Though she had not expected a response, she was utterly surprised to discover that
those who remained of the Eagle Clan were free
and lived some miles from New Town. They were
on the opposite side of the town from where Silver
Feather's clan lived.

Without telling Silver Feather, she had taken the
time to go to the Eagle Clan's village. Immediately
upon seeing the tension and mistrust in their eyes,
she had introduced herself to their chief. She knew
they had a right to be wary for she was the step-
daughter of the man who had taken so much from
them, including many lives.

But after she explained about the land and the
huge manor house, the chief quickly relaxed.

They had been so happy to learn that Silver Feather, the son of the man who was their chief so long ago, was alive and well, and was even a powerful chief now. There were immediate cheers and looks of delight in their dark eyes.

When she returned to Silver Feather's village, she was accompanied by those he had loved those long years ago. Silver Feather was stunned that it was happening.

He had been reunited with his people, and they all became reacquainted. He was especially happy to greet one man, who had been his best friend when they were children.

Red Hawk was currently chief of the Eagle Clan. But he knew that now that the whole clan was reunited, Silver Feather was the true chief. Silver Feather was the son of the chief they had all known and adored. And it was he who should have stepped fully into the chieftainship as soon as his father had died.

But that was so long ago.

Their lives had changed, as had their duties to a chief who they had been told had died after his escape on the day of his mother's and father's deaths. Colonel Jamieson Dettro had told them that he was dead and they should forget him.

But they had never forgotten.

Before the celebration began tonight, everyone met in the huge council house. Plans were made for the two clans to come together on the land that had once produced so much cotton. The mansion would be brought back to its original grandeur, but used in a different way.

Diana would set up a trading post there, where the Choctaw people could trade their lovely pelts, and even cotton, for the cotton fields would be revived and would make money for the Choctaw. The future looked promising for these combined Choctaw clans.

Diana didn't plan to live at Dettro Manor, though. She did not want to look as though she felt she was better than the other women of the tribe. Once married, she would share a Choctaw cabin with her husband. Their children would be raised in the Choctaw tradition.

She even felt more Choctaw than white now, even though she had yet to speak vows with her beloved.

But they would do so soon after the important Green Corn Ceremony was behind them.

"You were so good to search and find my chief's clan," Pretty Fawn whispered to Diana when there was a pause in the singing, as *tomfulla*, a dish made of fermented corn, was passed around, along with other delicious foods that had cooked all night over the women's cook fires.

Diana hadn't prepared anything for this celebration tonight, or for tomorrow's, for she had not yet had time to learn the art of cooking.

She was afraid that her inability to prepare even

the simplest of meals might disappoint Silver Feather, yet he had not outwardly shown any concern about it.

She would make him proud, soon, however, for Pretty Fawn had agreed to teach her everything that she needed to know to cook the same way as the other women.

"It was by chance that I found his Eagle Clan," Diana whispered back as she leaned closer to Pretty Fawn. "When I questioned the authorities about them at the courthouse, I truly did not expect a positive response. I was stunned when they immediately knew the answer to my question."

"It is sad that Silver Feather did not know sooner, yet had he, he might have gone to live with the Eagle Clan instead of staying with us," Pretty Fawn said, taking a platter of food, nodding a thank-you to the woman who handed it to her.

"Had he known where his clan was, I believe he would have done what he has done now," Diana answered. "He would have brought you all together as one heartbeat. That is the sort of man he is. He would never abandon those he loved."

Diana then gazed at Pretty Fawn's belly, which seemed to be a little larger today as the doeskin dress clung to it.

Then she smiled at Pretty Fawn. "I am so glad that your child is all right," she said. "Had you lost the child, I would have always felt responsible."

"I would not have allowed you to," Pretty Fawn

said, resting a hand gently on Diana's arm. "So do not think another thing about it. We are best friends. Best friends do not feel anything but love for one another."

"That *is* how I feel about you," Diana said, nodding. "And thank you for what you did for me this morning."

"The basket of herbs and roots?" Pretty Fawn asked innocently.

"Yes, those," Diana replied. "It was so sweet of you and your friends to make up a basket for me to replace those that I lost when Harry Braddock abducted me."

She smiled at Pretty Fawn. "And you even made certain that bluebells were in the basket since you know how much I adore them," she murmured. "Thank you, Pretty Fawn, I shall always remember such kindness."

At that moment, Silver Feather and White Cloud joined her and Pretty Fawn.

"Are you enjoying yourself tonight?" Silver Feather asked Diana. "Are you tired? All that traveling yesterday must have tired you."

"It did, yet I am so happy about the outcome that I don't feel the weariness yet in my bones," she said, laughing softly. She reached a gentle hand to his cheek. "My Silver Feather. I watched your eyes when your Eagle Clan came into the village, and how you so quickly knew who they were."

"It was not so much that I recognized them," Silver Feather said. "It was just a feeling that I had, especially when I looked at you and saw the radiance of your smile."

Diana smiled again in response. "And now you are all together again. Soon your villages will become one on the land that was taken from you. You will set up your village in the shadows of Dettro Manor." She laughed softly. "My stepfather is surely rolling over in his casket."

"His name does not deserve to be spoken aloud among my people," Silver Feather said, then realized his statement sounded like a reprimand. "I did not mean what I said to come out as though I am scolding you."

"I never take anything you say to me in a bad way," Diana said, smiling again. "So never feel as though you must guard what you say in my presence. Our bond is too strong for that."

Silver Feather took her hand and kissed its palm.

All became quiet when Two Winds, the great storyteller of the Eagle Clan, stood and began talking in a hypnotic tone. Diana became spellbound, for his tale seemed magical.

"Corn is our staff of life," he began. "Women enjoy a special relationship with the plant. According to Choctaw tradition, corn came to the Choctaw from a crow that had flown up from the south. The bird dropped a grain at the feet of a little girl, who asked, 'What is this?' Her mother came to investigate and determined that it was corn. In this way, the forefathers of the Choctaw got their seed corn. From that day forth, the women were in charge of the corn.

"To celebrate the corn, some of the ceremonies of our ancestors included the tick dance. The tick dance celebrated a Choctaw ambush of a European exploring party. To commemorate their victory over the boatload of Europeans, the first tick dancers traced out a sacred circle in the high grass on the riverbank adjacent to the boat and symbolically stomped on the ticks that crawled in the grass within their circle."

His stories went on and on, with the children moving closer and closer, their eyes wide with wonder.

And then a trace of dawn came along the horizon, marking the end of the first part of the Green Corn Ceremony.

Everyone would rest, and then the ceremony would begin anew when the sun waned and the moon appeared in its full brightness.

Diana went with Silver Feather into his cabin. She closed the door behind them, then turned to Silver Feather and twined her arms around his neck. "My love, I enjoyed the evening to its fullest, yet I could not help but keep thinking about being alone with you, for our own private celebration," she whispered. "I am so happy for you that the people of your Eagle Clan are outside making camp among the Turtle Clan. It seems somewhat surreal, doesn't it?"

"It is a miracle that came about because my woman cared enough to make it happen," Silver Feather said, smoothing Diana's hair back from her face. "Thank you, my Diana."

Diana was bone-tired, yet she still wanted to make love. She had felt the stirrings of desire within her soul from the moment she had seen the joy she had brought to her beloved's eyes when he saw his clan arriving at the village.

At that moment, she had never felt as close to anyone as she had to Silver Feather.

"Make love with me," she whispered against his lips. "I feel so much tonight. Do you feel it, too?"

"My heart is mended," he said throatily. "The part of my heart that always felt the absence of my true people has finally been put back together, making me whole again. Because of you, Diana. Because of you."

He swept her into his arms and carried her to his bedroom.

The glow from the huge outdoor fire sent its light into the room through the window, and along with the breaking dawn, it gave enough light for each to see the other as they disrobed.

Once fully unclothed, Silver Feather gently lowered Diana to his bed, soon stretching out above her, their bodies touching.

"This is the only true way to celebrate any-thing," Diana said, giggling, then sucked in a breath of sheer delight when he bent low and swept his tongue around one nipple of her breast and then the other.

She twined her fingers through his thick hair and drew him closer to her flesh, experiencing de-licious shivers of desire when he sucked one nip-ple and then the other, while one of his hands was suddenly between her legs, caressing her where she was wet and ready for him.

His lips came to hers, his mouth hot and sensu-ous.

As he caressed her and kissed her, Diana moaned, then sighed when he thrust inside her and began the rhythmic strokes that spun their usual golden web of magic around them.

He came to her, again and again, thrusting deeply, his arms around her, holding her against his hard body with his solid strength.

She clung to him as exquisite sensations spi-raled through her body.

He reverently breathed her name against her lips, then kissed her again, the curl of heat grow-ing in his body where passions lay smoldering just beneath the surface.

He kissed her slender throat, then leaned away from her so that he could absorb the wonders of her body, his eyes branding her.

Her body a river of sensations, Diana reached a

hand out and placed it at the nape of his neck, bringing his lips to hers again.

She sought his mouth with wild desperation, then felt that wondrous, magical heat claiming her.

She shuddered, arched, and cried out as his own body answered in kind.

As they lay there afterward, he rained kisses on her eyelids, and on her hair, then worshiped her flesh with his hands, caressing her where she had just felt the height of sensation.

"I am feeling it again," she cried out, trembling with readiness as he drove into her again, swiftly and surely.

His mouth sought hers, on fire with passion, seeking, probing, searching.

They clung together, their urgency building all over again, and then they rediscovered that wondrous place that made them aware of the depths of their love for one another, of their devotion.

This time, when it was over, they rolled away from each other, yet still held hands.

"It will be a marvelous day," Silver Feather said, smiling over at her, "when we come together as man and wife. There will be such a rejoicing inside my heart."

"Also mine," Diana murmured. "It is our destiny."

"Ours," he said, turning to her, framing her face between his hands. "We will finalize the Green

Corn Ceremony first, and then we will have our own special day."

"It is as though I am living in a fantasy world," Diana said softly.

He drew her into his arms and gave her a soft, sweet kiss before she drifted to sleep in his arms.

He eased her away from him.

Before covering her with a blanket, he sat there and gazed at her, adoring her. "My Diana, my Goddess of the Hunt," he whispered, then stretched out beside her for his own short nap before leaving his cabin again and resuming his duties as chief.

He snuggled against her and was soon asleep.

Chapter 29

If I worship one thing more than another,
It shall be the spread of my own body,
Or any part of it,
Translucent mold of me. . . .
It shall be yours!
— Walt Whitman

Diana was in the saddle of a white stallion. Silver Feather rode beside her on his own white steed, which Diana had gone into New Town and purchased for him with money that she had taken from the safe at Dettro Manor—money that she felt was hers. Everything in the manor was hers. All that lay outside it belonged to the Choctaw. But soon, it would jointly be Silver Feather's and Diana's, since they were going to be married.

She gazed over at him. The sun was a golden sheen on his copper face. His raven-black hair was flowing free down his bare, muscled back. He wore only a breechclout and moccasins on this, their wedding day, and she wore a new doeskin dress lavishly embellished with beautiful beads of many different colors.

Pretty Fawn had brought many dresses to Diana, her own private gifts to her new friend. All of them were new and had been stored away for future use. Pretty Fawn was gifted at sewing and spent a good portion of her day enjoying her craft.

There had been other gifts, mostly for Silver Feather, adored chief of his people. He had been given many eagle feathers and elk teeth, fine turquoise that shone like the summer sun, and several well-woven blankets richly adorned with the legends of his people.

But the most treasured gift of all was the white steed that Diana had given him, reminding him of those long years ago when he had said that he hoped to own such a horse when he grew up. Regardless that Silver Feather had his own white steed, it was the feelings behind the gift that made this horse more special than all the others. Diana recognized the pride in Silver Feather's eyes that came with riding tall in the saddle of the horse that she personally had picked out for him.

A sweet warmth rushed through her, and her heart was filled with much joy when she recalled the moment when she had presented the horse to Silver Feather.

She had just brought it into the village, to give to him, when she saw him leading another snow-white creature toward her. It was his wedding gift to her!

"I shall never forget the moment when I saw that you had acquired a white horse specifically for me, as I had purchased one for you," Diana said, drawing Silver Feather's eyes to her. "So much of our past has caught up to our present."

"You and I have been of one mind and heart since we first met, even when we were apart," Silver Feather said, taking her hand as she reached toward him. "It was destiny that brought us together again. Today we will seal that bond with marriage vows."

"I still can't believe this moment has finally come," Diana said, sliding her hand from his and holding her reins again. "But—"

"But what?" Silver Feather said, chuckling beneath his breath. He knew she was puzzled by his suggestion that they leave the village and have their wedding ceremony elsewhere.

Little did she know what lay ahead for her.

It would be such joy to watch her eyes light up when she saw everything that had been prepared for her.

"But I don't understand why we left the village," Diana said. "I thought you would want all of your people to share our bliss and to celebrate their chief taking a wife. Is this the way it is supposed to be? Do the couples always go away from the village when they are going to speak vows?"

"No, not always," Silver Feather said, shrugging slightly.

"Then why are we?" Diana persisted. "And why were your people in their lodges when we rode out of the village? I saw no one outside, not

even the elders, who usually sit around the outdoor fire sharing conversation and smokes. It is as
though your village shut down for the day. I am
truly confused. Is that a part of your tradition on
wedding days?"

"Be patient, my woman, and soon you shall
know the answers to your questions," Silver
Feather said, his eyes gleaming. "It will not be long
now."

Diana raised her eyebrows, looking puzzled.
She sighed heavily. "I am now even more confused."

"Be patient, my love. Patience is a virtue," Silver
Feather said. "You taught me that saying long
ago."

They rode onward in silence, and when they
reached a bend in the land, where trees grew thick,
Silver Feather reached out and took Diana's reins
and stopped her horse, then stopped his own.

"Why are we stopping?" Diana asked, her eyes
widening.

"We will leave our horses here and walk the rest
of the way," Silver Feather said.

"To where?" Diana asked, sliding down from
her saddle.

"Patience, remember. Patience," Silver Feather
said as he dismounted and tied their reins together
on the low limb of a tree.

"I am beginning to hate that word," Diana said,
her nerves rankled.

When they walked around the bend in the land and came out into the open, Diana gasped and stared.

"Now do you see why I asked you to practice patience?" Silver Feather said, chuckling. "Is this not something worth waiting for?"

"I can't believe my eyes," Diana murmured, awed by the trouble Silver Feather and his people had gone to in order to prepare this place for their chief's wedding.

In her whole life, including the time spent driving the stagecoach, she had never seen so many bluebells in one place.

This field of flowers reached as far as the eye could see, many more than she had seen on the hillside that fateful day.

"How . . . beautiful!" she exclaimed. "How absolutely, breathtakingly beautiful!"

The entire village of the Choctaw, both clans, were sitting in a half circle around a huge outdoor fire on the outer fringes of the bluebell field.

The tantalizing smells of many different foods wafted through the air, coming from the pots that were set amid the coals of the fire.

Children were sitting together in a cluster on one side, while the elders sat on the opposite side as though to show the comparison from young to old, with all the generations blending between.

Diana sorted through the people and found

Pretty Fawn. Her smile was radiant as she gazed back at Diana.

Pretty Fawn had helped prepare Diana for her wedding. She had brushed her hair until it shone, and she had gently painted a red path along the part in Diana's golden hair. The crown of wild-flowers that was perched atop Diana's head had been made by Pretty Fawn's delicate yet deft fingers.

Diana whispered a thank-you to Pretty Fawn now, as she had hugged her and thanked her over and over again earlier in the morning after Diana had slid into the loveliest of doeskin dresses.

"Did I not promise you bluebells on our wedding day?" Silver Feather said, sweeping a hand around her waist and guiding her toward a platform that had been placed to the left of his people.

"Yes, but not a whole field full of them," Diana said, almost giddy now from happiness. "But I do love them, Silver Feather." She smiled at him as they sat down on the platform. "And how I do love you."

"I have never loved as I love now," Silver Feather said, taking one of her hands. "Now enjoy what has been planned for us. It is a time for rejoicing, and my people are masters at knowing how to make that happen."

From somewhere to her far right, hidden amid the lush magnolia trees, drums made from the trunks of black gum trees began beating out their steady rhythm. The music of cane flutes and gourd rattles filled with pebbles accompanied them.

Women dressed in grass skirts appeared from what seemed nowhere and began whirling around, dancing in time with the music that flowed, ascending and descending.

"These dancers are called Grass Dancers," Silver Feather whispered to Diana. "Watch as others join them now. Those dancers are called Jingle Dress Dancers."

The Jingle Dress Dancers' outfits grabbed Diana's attention. Their dresses were made of a bright calico print, with large tin cone "jingles," which the Choctaw called bells, sewn on them.

As they danced, their feet lifted in a hopping fashion and their bodies rocked, causing the jingles to produce a rhythmic, clacking sound.

And just as Diana was beginning to enjoy the performance, both the Jingle Dress Dancers and the Grass Dancers left, to be replaced by men wearing smoked-hide leggings and capes. The dancers' buckskin fringes swayed, and their hawk-and-eagle-feather bustles fluttered in the breeze.

As they spun and twisted, more women joined them again, this time wearing fancy embroidered shawls with long fringes to accentuate their movements.

All of the dancers used intricate, fast, and acrobatic motions as they strained and whirled and turned in a dazzling explosion of color and high-stepping spins.

And then suddenly the music stopped and the dancers were gone, as though they had disappeared into thin air.

But soon Diana saw them all return and join the others around the fire, their regular clothes on now, their costumes left behind somewhere.

Silver Feather stood up and turned to Diana. He held a hand out to her. "It is time to complete our bond," he said thickly. "Come, my Diana, my Goddess of the Hunt."

Her heart racing, her eyes bright, Diana smiled at Silver Feather and took his hand. They walked to the field of bluebells and stood amid the flowers, facing one another, as the people stood to watch and listen.

"Diana, I love you and marry you today, not only for what you have always been to me but for what you gave to me and made me be," Silver Feather said, his eyes taking Diana in, feeling her deep inside his soul. "My woman, since the early years of our lives, when we met and fell in love, you have never lost your loveliness, your sweetness. I will love you, forever—my woman, my wife."

Diana thrilled through and through to know that she was now Silver Feather's wife. His words had touched her soul.

"My Silver Feather, I love you and marry you

today, as we planned, it seems, a whole lifetime ago," Diana said, tears hot at the corners of her eyes and her happiness so intense and complete. "Our hearts have always beat as one, and that has never been as true as it is today. We are in the springtime of our lives, the light of a lifetime together still ahead of us. Although fate parted us, destiny has brought us together again. My husband, I shall be everything you want me to be—a wife, a mother, a companion, and all else that a woman can be to a man. Silver Feather, my all is given to you today, our wedding day. I love you, love you, love you!"

Touched to the very core of his being by what she professed, Silver Feather felt his own tears burning at the corners of his eyes. He swept Diana into his arms and gave her a soft, quivering kiss.

They stepped away from each other as the crowd cheered and clapped. They sang in honor of their chief's having taken a bride.

Pretty Fawn stepped up to them. "Diana, come with me," she said softly, as White Cloud took Silver Feather by the arm. The two led both of them away from the crowd.

They walked until they reached the far side of the bluebell field, away from the great outdoor fire and the Choctaw people, where a new cabin had been built.

Pretty Fawn and White Cloud stepped away from Silver Feather and Diana. They clasped their hands together, their eyes brimming with happiness as they looked from one to the other, then back again.

"Your people will feast and celebrate your marriage as you rejoice for the rest of the day in total privacy," White Cloud said. He looked mischievously into the chief's eyes. "Tomorrow is the hunt, my chief. Do not tire yourself so much tonight that you cannot notch your bow with an arrow tomorrow!"

Silver Feather laughed softly, then turned and went inside the cabin with Diana, closing the door behind them.

As the embers of the fire in a fireplace made of stones cast their light into the curling shadows, what Diana saw made her gasp in wonder.

It was only one room, obviously built for two lovers. There was no furniture, only rich pelts, blankets, and pots of food sitting close to the fire, sending out tantalizing aromas.

But the one quilt that Diana saw made her heart melt. She flung herself into her husband's arms. "You found my mother's special patchwork quilt made of her dresses," she said, gazing lovingly into his eyes. "You brought it here for our night together."

"I remembered how you loved that quilt, and after we took possession of the manor, I went into the passageways while you were with Pretty Fawn preparing for our marriage. I searched until I found the quilt," he said softly. "My wife, it was in that same small trunk in the passageway that you placed there the last time we were together."

"Yes, I remember," Diana said, her voice catching. "And that you remembered how special it was to me, so much that you sought it out and found it, means more to me than you will ever know."

"I want to make your each and every day happy and memorable," Silver Feather said, searching her eyes. "And . . . your nights."

"*Our* nights, don't you mean?" Diana said, reaching up to gently stroke his face.

Silver Feather stepped away from her and lifted the crown of flowers from her hair.

"And what else are you going to remove?" Diana teased, as she placed her hands at the waist of his breechclout. "I have less to remove from you than you do me."

"And that was purposely planned," Silver Feather said, sucking in a wild breath as she slowly slid the breechclout down his body, her hand glancing along his manhood, causing it to grow to its full length.

"Now look what you did," Silver Feather said, his eyes dark pools of passion.

"That is only the beginning," Diana teased. "Just you wait and see. . . ."

Chapter 30

When'er the fate of those I hold most dear
Tells to my fearful breast a tale of sorrow,
O bright-eyed Hope,
My morbid fancy cheer,
Let me awhile thy sweetest comforts sorrow.
                                        —John Keats

Outside the music and dancing continued, but inside the cabin Silver Feather and Diana rejoiced in their marriage, in their being together for the rest of their lives.

"Dreams are what brought us together again," Silver Feather said as he knelt over Diana, his eyes dark with passion. "Had I not dreamed about my people's spiritual bone house, we would never have had that chance meeting. Had the bones not been stolen, I would have gone there and prayed, then returned to my people and continued life as it had been without you."

"Had I not chosen to drive a stagecoach, we never would have met either," Diana murmured, trembling with excitement as Silver Feather leaned low and brushed kisses across her breasts. "When I realized where that stagecoach run was taking me, I was assailed by memories of you. I hesitated to accept that assignment, for I feared the ache of loneliness for you that would come with my arrival at Dettro Manor."

"But we both went, and here we are now, man and wife, with a lifetime of happiness together ahead of us," Silver Feather said, his hands moving over her, awakening her every sensitive place to an ecstasy that only he could create.

"And children," Diana whispered against his lips.

"Yes. And children," he whispered back to her, enfolding her with his solid strength. His muscled arms around her, he lifted her body up snugly against his. "We will have many to help assure my people's future, for it is the children who are the hope of our future. To multiply now is to help save our people's heritage later."

"Then let us make a child tonight," Diana whispered, twining her arms around his neck. "I am ready for you, my love."

Silver Feather reached down and wove his fingers through the soft, curly tendrils of golden hair at the juncture of her thighs. He caressed her there, feeling her trembling with passion. Then he kissed her hungrily as he thrust himself inside her.

He wrapped his arms around her again and drew her close, reveling in the sweet, warm press of her body against his. Aware of the exquisite sensations spiraling through her body, and a keen happiness bubbling from deep within her, Diana moaned against his lips, her arms locked around his neck, her body moving with his.

His body a river of emotions, heating more with each new thrust inside her, Silver Feather slid his lips from hers and moved downward until he found a breast. He rained kisses across it, then flicked her nipple with his tongue, drawing renewed groans from within her.

He loved the yielding silk of her womanhood as he drove into her more swiftly and surely. The heat in his loins was spreading, sending a fiery awareness throughout his body.

"I love you so," he whispered against her lips.

He held her close as his fingers pressed urgently into her flesh. On fire with passion, his mouth sought hers, his tongue seeking, searching, probing.

With a moan of ecstasy, Diana returned his kiss. Clinging to him, she locked her legs around him and drew him even more deeply within her.

He entwined his fingers in her hair, then moved to her breasts again, stroking, caressing.

Never had Diana felt Silver Feather so caught up in the passion of their lovemaking. He wrapped her within his arms again, crushing her to him so hard that she gasped. His mouth bore down upon hers, exploding with a renewed raw passion.

All of these things, all the truth of his love for her, caused bright threads of wonder to weave through her heart.

She clung.

She rocked.

She sighed.

And then they reached that place that gave them the ultimate pleasure. They quivered and quaked against one another, both clinging desperately, their lips on fire as they kissed with abandon.

When it was over, they lay side by side, breathing hard, their bodies covered with a sheen of perspiration against the glow of the fire.

Diana gazed around her, becoming aware of the preponderance of bluebells. She reached over and picked up one of the flowers.

Smiling, she leaned up on an elbow and began tracing Silver Feather's body with the flower, giggling as she saw an occasional tremor of what she knew was a renewed passion.

Mischievously, she continued to trace the muscled contours of his body until she came to that part of his anatomy that had the skills of making her aware of being a woman.

So often, when she was wearing men's clothes, she had doubted that she could ever truly be a woman again, wearing pretty things, being with a man, loving him.

In those days, thinking about the possibility of falling in love—if ever she was given the chance under the strange circumstances of her life—she had never been able to banish the hope that it would be Silver Feather.

She would recall just how handsome he had been as a young brave. She knew even then that his future as chief was far from possible since his clan was enslaved.

"When you found a people who took you in, did you see yourself as possibly being a chief after all?" Diana voiced her thoughts. She took her hand from his body for a moment.

"I was just so glad to find people of my tribe who would take me in, that I did not think beyond that," Silver Feather said, sitting up and sliding a log onto the fire.

He turned to her. He reached out for her and took her hands in his, then led her onto his lap so that she straddled and faced him.

"I had dreams of being a chief one day. Oftentimes as a young brave, my dreams would come to pass," he said. "I dreamed of being a great leader like my father had been. I vowed to myself never to allow whites to fool me into believing them. I am proud to have kept my Turtle Clan safe from whites. And I am relieved that my true clan is with me again, among them, cousins I had not thought I would ever see again."

"You have it all now, Silver Feather," Diana said. "You have your people back, your land, and . . ."

"And you," he said, completing her sentence. "I feel great joy about these recent blessings. It was the Great One Above that brought me to this place in my life, and you to yours. It is with much gratitude that I say my morning prayers, for everything is as it should be."

"When are you going to move your people back to the land that has long been denied you?" Diana asked, leaning against him, loving the feel of his skin against hers. "Are you going to plant cotton?"

"Yes, there will be cotton plants, for I know the money it can bring to those who harvest it, since I witnessed it firsthand through your stepfather," Silver Feather replied. "He did this from greed. I will do it only as a way to better my people and make them stronger against any future intrusion from whites."

"I confess, I'm greedy," Diana said, smiling into his eyes. "But my greed has nothing to do with money. It all has to do with you."

"Then I shall feed your needs, my woman," Silver Feather said, softly kissing her lips. Diana could feel the first stirring of his arousal.

He gazed at her with eyes that looked smoky. "You are so beautiful," he said huskily. "Your eyes, your lips, your body, are all an incredible beautiful dream, a dream that is real to me now, not only imagined. My Diana, oh, my Diana, how I have loved you for so long, and will, for an eternity."

"As I will always love you," she whispered back, smiling up at him as he spread her legs, then thrust himself inside her moist, warm place.

As their bodies pressed together, he began his rhythmic strokes, thrusting endlessly deeper as their lips came together in an explosive, quivering kiss.

This time the ultimate pleasure was reached quickly. Diana's gasps became long, soft whimpers as she strained her hips up to him, taking him in as far as he could reach.

He held her tightly as the heat spread throughout him, the flames lapping at his loins.

He felt it growing to the bursting point.

Then there was a great shuddering in his loins.

Diana clung tightly to him and cried out at her fulfillment as he did the same, their bodies soon subsiding, exhausted, into each other.

Breathing hard, their bodies still trembling from their second ecstasy, they lay there, their hands clasped.

Soon shouts and laughter intruded on the quiet cabin. Startled, Diana pulled away from Silver Feather and looked at the closed door.

She turned to him. "What are they doing?" she asked, her eyebrows raised. "I thought all that was left of the celebration was eating."

"Sometimes that isn't enough when my—our— people are brought together for any sort of ceremony or celebration," Silver Feather said.

He, too, looked toward the door, remembering a time when he was as young as those who were probably participating in the ball game now being played beneath the moon.

"They are participating in a Choctaw ball game," he told her. His eyes danced. "Do you want to go and watch, or stay here and eat, then make love again?"

"I would like to go for a little while, then return to eat, and, ah, yes, make love again," Diana answered with a shy smile. "If we are going to make a baby, we must be diligent."

"Then let us go and see who is the winner tonight," Silver Feather said, hurrying into his breechclout, as Diana pulled the beautiful dress over her head, then slipped her feet into moccasins.

"Will it look strange that we are leaving our cabin so soon?" Diana asked, now hesitating.

"Nothing we choose to do on our wedding night will look strange to anyone. It is our night to do with as we please," Silver Feather said. He took her hand. "Come. We shall go and share in the fun."

Hand in hand, they returned to the celebration, only to find that most of the people had left the outdoor fire. They were in an open meadow, opposite where the flowers were growing in their lovely blue expanse.

She was surprised by how the young braves were dressed. She didn't recognize what sort of

tails were affixed to the backs of their breechclouts.
But whatever it was made them look animallike.

"I see you wondering about what the young
men are wearing," Silver Feather said, standing
with her and some of his clansmen who were ob-
serving the ball game. Others preferred to sit
around the fire, talking and eating, while the elders shared smokes with their long-stemmed
pipes.

"Yes, they look mystical," Diana said, gazing
questioningly up at Silver Feather.

"The young braves have affixed wildcat tails to
the backs of their breechclouts. It is said that such
decoration imbues them with the ferocity of the
wildcat," he said, then nodded toward their ball
sticks. "You see, too, the white dove feathers that
are tied to their ball sticks?"

"I saw the feathers but wasn't sure what sort
they were," Diana answered, turning her eyes
again toward the game. The boys were playing
hard and with ferocity as a ball was batted around,
caught, and then batted again.

She smiled up at Silver Feather. "Our sons will
be participating in these same games. Can't you
see them now? They will look exactly like you did
at the age I first met you. They will remind me of
those times we spent together in the passageways." She clutched his arm. "Oh, Silver Feather, I
am so hoping to have sons!"

"And daughters," Silver Feather said, before

getting lost in the game. He watched the young men competing, for he knew each one as well as he would know his own sons. The Choctaw chiefs always kept a close bond with all Choctaw youth, especially the young braves, who were the promise of their tribe. If they were not taught the right road of life, then all of the Choctaw would be lost.

Diana noticed how intently he was watching the ball game. She turned her attention back to the young men. She was soon caught up in rooting for them, without choosing any particular boy to root for.

When the games concluded, the young braves hugged each other and laughed. None of them seemed to be so competitive that he could not enjoy the victory of the others.

Diana gazed around her. Everyone seemed unaware that their chief was among them. She thought it might be because they did not want to interfere in his night with his bride, for tomorrow everything would change.

Tomorrow both clans of Choctaw were going to be uprooted to move onto the land that had been taken from them those long years ago.

Suddenly Diana's heart skipped a beat as she looked up and saw a bright orange glow in the sky in the distance. She looked quickly over at Silver Feather, who had also just caught sight of it.

"Your village?" she gasped.

"No, it is too far to be our village," he said

tightly. "I fear it might be something else. From here, we're closer to Dettro Manor."

"But there are other manors—" Diana said, hoping that what he was suggesting was not true. She still had to sort through her mother's things, including the trunk that contained the diary.

"There are no manors or plantations between here and Dettro Plantation," he said. "But perhaps I am wrong."

"Even though this is our wedding night, Silver Feather, I need to go and see whether Dettro Manor is burning," she said, swallowing hard.

Silver Feather took her by the shoulders and turned her to face him. "My wife, we both are concerned about what we are witnessing. I, too, wish to know if our land has been intruded upon again."

"Who would do this?" Diana asked. "Those who were involved in the button trade are in jail."

Then she blanched. "Except for—"

"The man who begged to be set free because his wife was with child?" Silver Feather remembered the man well.

"Chief, I see the sky lit up with fire!" White Cloud said, running to him.

Others came with the same news.

"We will investigate!" he cried.

"I will go, too," Diana said, walking quickly to where they had left their horses.

"It might be dangerous," Silver Feather said,

stopping her with a hand on her shoulders. "You are now my wife, not a stagecoach driver. Perhaps you should stay with the women."

"You know I can't do that," she said quietly so the others wouldn't hear. "Please don't ask that of me. I could not just sit idly by and wait for your return. Surely you know that."

"Yes, I do," Silver Feather said, smiling at her. "So, yes, come with us."

She flung herself into his arms and hugged him, then hurried to mount her beautiful white stallion as Silver Feather leaped onto his.

The other warriors had to return home for their steeds, but Diana and Silver Feather could not bear to wait for them. They rode on, alone.

"They will soon catch up with us," Silver Feather shouted to her.

She nodded, her eyes watching the dancing orange shadows in the sky.

Chapter 31

Breast that presses against other breasts,
It shall be you!
My brain it shall be your
Occult convolution.

—Walt Whitman

With Silver Feather and Diana in the lead, the warriors had pressed hard into the night until they came to the edge of the plantation grounds.

Silver Feather and Diana wheeled their horses to a stop when they saw the glowing embers on the ground, the only remains of what had once been the most magnificent plantation house in the entire area.

Like ghosts in the night, four tall stone chimneys soared out of the rubble.

The other warriors drew their horses up beside Silver Feather and Diana.

"We must not go any farther on our horses," Silver Feather said, already dismounting. He grabbed his rifle from the gunboot. "If the one who did this is still in the area, we do not want him to know that we have arrived."

Everyone dismounted and tethered their horses' reins on low tree limbs.

Then arming themselves as well, the warriors crept slowly and quietly with Silver Feather and Diana along the edge of the live oak forest, still not going out into the open.

As Diana followed Silver Feather, her own pistol in her right hand, she was in shock, unable even to react to what she saw. Then she swallowed back a sob that came from the flood of memories of those years with her mother, and the time with Silver Feather and their adventures as they had played in the passageways of Dettro Manor.

It was all gone now.

All that remained was a pile of glowing orange ash.

She grabbed Silver Feather by an arm. "Silver Feather, you know that the fire was intentionally set. How else could it have begun?"

"I believe that the word has spread among the white community that we Choctaw have reclaimed what was denied us for so long," Silver Feather replied. "Someone who resents a people with copper skin owning such a fine house and land might have done this to frighten us away or to prove that no matter what the papers show, the land can still be taken from us."

"You think it was done because of prejudices?" Diana asked, gazing over at him, seeing a mixture of anger and hurt in his eyes.

Diana wondered if it had been done to settle the score over what Silver Feather had done about the bones. He had stopped a business that had brought much money into many white men's pockets.

As before, her thoughts went back to the one man who might have had a role in this—the only one who had not been arrested with the others.

Earl Sharp!

Then she remembered all those men and women who had been allowed to go home after they left the factory. Until now they had not entered her mind. But perhaps among them were some who became enraged when they realized their livelihood had been taken from them.

Diana's head was spinning with all of these possibilities.

She looked up to see White Cloud approaching Silver Feather.

"The one who did this is surely long gone by now," he said in a low, angry growl.

"Yes, I am sure you are right," Silver Feather replied. "I doubt that we shall ever know who is to blame."

"We still have the land," White Cloud said. "The house would have been a good trading post."

"But the fact that someone destroyed it, came on land of the Choctaw and again wronged us, is something that I cannot get past," Silver Feather said. "Will it ever end?"

"No, as long as there are Choctaw on this earth with fire in their blood and air in their lungs, it will not end," White Cloud said, his eyes narrowing in anger.

Startled, Diana turned quickly when she caught a movement at her far right side, where another stand of tall live oaks grew.

There! She saw it again. Someone was standing amid the trees. It was a man.

The glowing embers revealed a man standing in the shadows, though she could not make out his facial features.

The man seemed transfixed by the fire. So intent was he upon what he was seeing, he was not aware of the Choctaw warriors being near.

She had heard about people who started fires in order to stand back and watch the flames. It was a disease called pyromania.

She had never actually known anyone with the disease, but even to know that there were such people on this earth made her feel ill in her stomach.

If this man had happened upon the grand old manor standing vacant, maybe he had seen an opportunity to set the house aflame in order to watch it burn. If that was the case, this was not done to purposely wrong the Choctaw.

It was his sickness that caused the fire to be set. Nothing more.

As one of the stone fireplaces tumbled over into

the embers, flickering ash sprayed high into the air, shedding enough light for Diana to recognize the face of the man. She gasped and clutched her throat.

"My Lord, it's Earl!" She grabbed Silver Feather by an arm. "Silver Feather, look over there! It's Earl! He's watching the fire. See how strange he looks? How he seems actually to enjoy seeing the house burn? He is surely a pyromaniac."

Silver Feather's fingers tightened on his rifle. "White Cloud, circle around behind him. We cannot chance his escape. He has much to answer for, and this time if he lies . . ."

His voice trailed off.

He gave Diana a wavering glance, then they and the others made a wide swing around behind Earl, closing in on all sides. When they were close enough for Earl to hear their approach, everyone stopped.

Silver Feather nodded to those who were directly behind him, leading them on around to Earl's left side. He directed others around to his right and others to stand directly behind him.

Then Silver Feather and Diana suddenly stepped out into the open. Earl was startled. He dropped his rifle. His eyes were wide as he looked from one to the other.

"Where did you come from?" he asked shakily, inching back away from them. "And why are you lookin' at me like that?"

"How could you ask such a question?" Diana said before Silver Feather got a chance to say anything back to him. "You started the fire. You did it to get back at Silver Feather when you heard he reclaimed this land and house. Or did you set the fire just to enjoy watching the flames?"

"You have me wrong on all counts," Earl stammered.

"Raise your hands," Silver Feather said, motioning with his rifle toward Earl. "Now!"

"No, Earl, I believe I am right on all counts," Diana said. "Don't try and cast the blame on anyone else."

"I came along—and—and—saw it," Earl stammered. "I stopped to watch, that's all."

"Why would you want to watch something as terrible as a home burning?" Diana asked, aching anew inside her heart when she thought of all that was lost to her because of the fire.

Earl gulped hard and lowered his eyes.

Silver Feather went to him and grabbed him by the throat. "Tell me the truth," he hissed. "I cannot stand a liar. They are the worst lot of men on this earth."

"I have never lied to you," Earl said, his eyes wild as he tried to wrestle Silver Feather's hand away from his throat. "Stop it. You're strangling me."

"Now that isn't a bad idea, is it?" Diana said. "You deserve no better treatment."

"Admit to your lies," Silver Feather said. He tightened his grip.

Earl's face turned crimson red.

His fingers desperately clawed at Silver Feather's hand.

"I . . . am . . . not a liar," Earl gasped. "Let . . . me . . . go. Please. Let me go."

"Tell the truth, or stand here the rest of the night with my hand at your throat. But know this—my grip will tighten more and more until you find it hard to get any breath inside your lungs," Silver Feather said flatly.

He squeezed even harder.

"All right, I—I am guilty of lying," Earl stammered. "I—I confess to having lied. But not the lie you are saying that I am guilty of."

"I am waiting to hear the truth, then," Silver Feather said flatly. "Speak, white man. It is time for all truths!"

"Let go of my throat and I'll tell you everything," Earl choked out. His eyes pleaded with Silver Feather. "Please?"

Silver Feather saw and heard the pleading. He could recall a time when his people had been forced to beg. It made him uncomfortable to see any man beg—even a white man who had just confessed to being a liar.

He dropped his hand. He watched as Earl rubbed his raw skin, his lungs heaving as he took deep breaths.

"Speak!" Silver Feather shouted. "Now!"

"I lied to you when I said that I had a wife with child," Earl gulped out. "I had to. I didn't want to be handed over to Sheriff Duffy. He is a mean son of a gun."

"You lied about that?" Diana gasped. "How could you?"

"'Cause it would save my life, that's why," Earl said. His eyes glistened. "Sometimes lies are necessary."

"What does that have to do with your being here?" Silver Feather asked, tightening his grip on his rifle.

"I came to settle a score with Harry Braddock, that's why," Earl said tightly.

"What sort of score?" Diana asked. "What did he do to you?"

"He scared the livin' daylights outta me, that's what," Earl said, shuddering.

"How?" Diana persisted.

Earl hung his head, then looked guardedly at Silver Feather. "I came and told him what you'd done about causin' the delivery of bones to be stopped. I expected good payment for the information. He paid me, all right. He drew a gun on me and pretended he was going to kill me."

"But I see he didn't shoot you," Diana said sarcastically.

"Naw, but I couldn't get that moment off my mind," Earl said, his eyes narrowing angrily. "And he didn't pay me a red cent for the information. So I came tonight and showed him a thing or two. I set his house afire. I hope he died in the flames. He deserved no less'n that. He wasn't worth anything, you know."

"And so you set the fire for that reason?" Silver Feather said, searching Earl's eyes for the truth. "To get back at him?"

"Yep, and as you see, I did a damn good job," Earl said, with a strange sort of cackling laugh.

"And so you think you killed Harry Braddock, do you?" Diana said, placing her fists on her hips.

"I'm certain he died," Earl said, nodding. "Otherwise, he'd be out here, wouldn't he? He'd be gunnin' for me. Nope, he can't hurt anyone ever again."

"Harry Braddock will not be, as you say, gunning for anyone anytime soon," Silver Feather said. "But not because you set this house aflame. A house that—by the way—belonged to me, not Harry Braddock. You set fire to my home."

"What?" Earl gasped incredulously.

"Papers were found that proved that all of this land and the house belong to my Choctaw people," Silver Feather said, smiling smugly.

"You ain't foolin' with me?" Earl gulped. "It was truly your home?"

"Exactly," Diana said, folding her arms across her chest. "You were caught red-handed burning a house that belonged to the Choctaw, not Harry Braddock."

"I'll be damned," Earl said, then paled. "I'm— I'm—damn sorry."

"You have no idea what you took from the Choctaw—and me—when you set fire to this house," Diana said, remembering those wonderful days with Silver Feather in the passageways. She had wanted to share them with their children.

And she had wanted to go to the attic to retrieve some of her mother's belongings.

"At least Harry Braddock is dead," Earl said, a little too smugly.

"And you'll take the credit for that?" Diana asked, taking a step toward him.

"Yep, seems so," Earl said, his eyes brightening. "Sorry 'bout the house, but glad about the man!"

"You didn't kill Harry," Diana explained. "He wasn't in the house."

"How do you know that?" Earl said, his eyes widening.

"Because he was already dead," Silver Feather said dryly.

"What? When did this happen?" Earl asked, shocked.

"A few nights ago. So you won't be taken into custody by Sheriff Duffy for taking someone's life, but you will be taken away for setting fire to Dettro Manor and for your role in stealing the bones," Silver Feather said flatly.

"But you let me go earlier," Earl whined.

"You should have stayed away," Silver Feather said. He grabbed Earl by the throat again. "You are not a smart man, are you?"

Earl glared at him. "I wish I'd come after you, not Harry Braddock," he said venomously. "I hate all redskins. Go ahead and kill me, Injun."

"It would be too easy on you," Silver Feather said, dropping his hand. "You will join the others in the jail at New Town. You will pay at the hands of white people."

He shoved Earl away from him and motioned to White Cloud. "Take him away," he said darkly. "I cannot stand to look at him."

"I've settled a few scores, anyway, by burning the house," Earl shouted as he was half dragged away. "No Injun will ever live in it."

"He's a lunatic," Diana said. "A raving lunatic."

"What I do not like is that he deceived me much too easily with his lies. I believed him when he told us of a wife with child," Silver Feather said, frowning. "I cannot allow such things to happen, or I will look like a weak leader. I must be able to see truth and lies when I am faced with them."

"No one can be perfect," Diana said soothingly, taking one of Silver Feather's hands. "Not even you, my darling."

He smiled wanly at her. "Well, maybe not, but I know a woman who is nearly perfect in all ways," he said, taking her in his arms. "You, my wife. You."

She clung to him. "I am so sorry about all of this. You will see. It will get better. We'll clear this land of the ruins of the house. It will give us more space for the cotton plants. I see a bright future for us all."

"There will always be someone who tries to stand in the way of our progress," Silver Feather said, then walked her to their horses, where the warriors were saddled and waiting.

White Cloud and another warrior had already left with Earl, traveling toward New Town.

The others followed Silver Feather and Diana as they rode homeward.

"The hunt is tomorrow. After that we will center our attention on moving our people to the land that is now legally ours," Silver Feather said. "It will be a fine place to grow not only cotton but also the green corn that we depend on for our food."

"Tomorrow I will show you how skilled I am at hunting," Diana said, smiling at him. "I will prove myself worthy of the title of Goddess of the Hunt."

He reached over, drew her close, and kissed her.

"My Diana," he said huskily. "How did I ever exist without you?"

Chapter 32

Out of your whole life
give but a moment.
—Robert Browning

In the forest, bittersweet and porcelainberry grew as tall as the tallest trees, creating a dense and heavy foliage. The weight of the vines had pulled down a tree directly in the path where Silver Feather and Diana were traveling.

The only weapon Silver Feather carried with him today was a bow and a quiver of arrows, while Diana had a rifle.

The sun could scarcely be seen through the leaves overhead as Diana and Silver Feather led their steeds around the fallen tree.

"I was so surprised when you told me that you and I would be going on the hunt today," Diana commented. "I had thought that the warriors were going. Didn't you say this was the final hunt before moving our village to the plantation and that this hunt was necessary to replenish the food supply before clearing the land?"

"Yes, I said that, and, yes, my warriors are hunting, but somewhere away from our private hunt," Silver Feather said, noticing how she was dressed today.

She wore a smoked-buckskin garment, which would hold up better than doeskin for a day of riding and hunting. The dress reached only just past her knees, where the fringe fluttered even now as the breeze swept through the forest in its cool dampness. She wore knee-high moccasins for protection should she and Silver Feather come upon any snakes in the forest. Her hair hung in one long golden braid down her back.

Silver Feather, too, wore his raven-black hair in a big braid. He had dressed in a full outfit of the same sort of buckskin, his leggings tucked into the same kind of high moccasins. His bow was slung over his left shoulder. His quiver of arrows lay against his back on his right side.

"I don't understand," Diana said, confused about his decision to hunt in such a way. She had looked forward to watching the warriors track and bring down game, as she hoped to be able to bring home her own deer. Diana was skilled with a rifle. Her stepfather had taught her to be a crack shot, and it had been necessary for her to refine that skill since she had only herself for protection while driving the stagecoaches.

"My wife, a true hunt is not the place for a woman," Silver Feather said. "It is actually taboo.

All warriors see the presence of a woman as bad luck."

"Then why do you have me with you?" Diana said, her eyes revealing the hurt that she felt over being considered bad luck. "Am I not going to bring you bad luck?"

"I could never see you as taboo," Silver Feather said, finally having ridden around the fallen tree and now able to move straight ahead again, where the trees were thinner. "And, no, you could never bring me bad luck. But that is because you are my wife and I trust you in all things. My warriors would see you as an interference, if not as taboo."

"But, then, why are you here with me instead of with your warriors?" Diana persisted.

"Did not we plan long ago to go on a special hunt together when we were older?" Silver Feather asked back.

"Yes, but that was so long ago," Diana answered. "Many things have changed."

"This is now, my wife, and we are fulfilling a promise," Silver Feather said. "We are on a hunt together. You are my true Goddess of the Hunt today."

"I suddenly don't feel like a goddess of anything," Diana said, pouting.

"I did not mean to make you feel bad about this," Silver Feather said, coming to a halt.

Diana stopped beside him, and Silver Feather

sidled his horse closer to hers. He gently placed a hand on her face.

"My Diana, I have not deceived you. I had no choice but to bring you on the hunt alone. Too many of my warriors spoke against you joining the larger hunt. I understood their concern. I wish that you would."

"I'm sorry if I am behaving like a spoiled brat," Diana said, suddenly aware of just how she was acting.

"A spoiled brat?" Silver Feather said, raising an eyebrow. "I have never heard anyone described that way."

Diana laughed softly. "It is just a way to describe someone who isn't being very nice." She took his hand and held it. "I'm sorry. I never want to disappoint you."

"You never could," Silver Feather said. "And you are not a 'spoiled brat.' You are everything that is sweet on this earth, Diana. And I can understand how confused you must be."

"I wanted to prove to you that I *could* hunt," Diana said, smiling at him. "Although I have to admit, I have never killed anything in my life."

They rode again beside one another.

"Please tell me about the hunt. What is the most coveted hide that you seek?" Diana asked. "I want to learn everything about your people, even such things as this."

"Deer is the most important to the Choctaw,"

Silver Feather said. "Bear skins are the second most prized in trade. All in all, there are deer, bear, fox, and wildcat skins, as well as beaver pelts."

He looked ahead again. "Another important commodity traded is tallow, but it never overtook beeswax in candle manufacturing. Beeswax is worth twice as much per pound," he said, sounding as though he was in deep thought.

"I never considered beeswax as a trade item," Diana said, then flinched and looked quickly away from him when she heard a sudden sound to their far left.

Silver Feather had heard it too, but he didn't take an arrow from his quiver. This was Diana's time.

His eyes dancing, and with a half smile on his lips, he watched her as she placed a hand on her rifle, close by in her gunboot.

Diana's heart raced at the thought of what might be expected of her in the next moment or two. She was a crack shot, but she had never shot at anything alive, only tin cans and bottles during target practice.

If she was actually faced with a living thing, she doubted that she could kill it.

But she had to give it her best effort, for she had promised Silver Feather that she would go on a hunt with him. She was his Goddess of the Hunt, wasn't she? But going on a hunt and actually shooting something were two different things. She felt sick at the pit of her stomach when she thought about killing a beautiful deer—or anything else, for that matter.

"A deer," Silver Feather said, remaining still. "See through that brush? It's feeding on the grass at the edge of that lake yonder. There are not only one but two. You can have the first chance, Diana. Let us dismount and get closer, but we must be quiet. A deer's perception is keen, and the wind can take our scent to it."

Her heart pounding, Diana dreaded being there and what might be expected of her. She dismounted along with Silver Feather.

Silver Feather watched her take the rifle from the gunboot. He motioned her to follow him through the thick brush.

"Try and walk lightly," he whispered to her. "We must make no sound."

Diana gulped hard and nodded at him. She moved alongside him, her knees weak from fear. She wanted to prove herself to her husband. If she didn't actually go through with this, she might look weak.

She felt guilty for drawing him away from the true hunt just because she wanted to go, too.

"Quietly," Silver Feather whispered again as they got as close as they dared, then knelt behind a thick stand of bushes.

Diana slowly shoved some branches aside. She

had a clear view of one of the deer. The other had disappeared from sight.

"Slowly," Silver Feather whispered to her. "Slowly lift your rifle."

Again Diana gulped hard, and the deer became fuzzy as she peered at it. Suddenly Diana realized she was crying. Tears had sprung forth at the thought of killing something as beautiful as that deer.

It jerked its head up.

Diana's knees had turned to water, and her heart pounded like drums inside her chest as the deer turned its eyes in their direction, as though it sensed they were there.

Diana looked through her haze of tears directly into the dark, round eyes of the deer. She blinked her eyes as she aimed through the brush, then felt too sick at her stomach to continue.

She yanked the rifle back, sat down and placed the weapon on the ground, then buried her face in her hands. "I can't," she choked out. "I can't kill it. It's—it's—too beautiful. How can anyone . . . ?"

Seeing how torn she was, and understanding how she felt, Silver Feather removed his bow and dropped it to the ground, then knelt before Diana. He framed her face with his hands, and brought her eyes up to his.

"You do not have to shoot anything, ever," he told her. "I understand."

"Do you?" Diana murmured, searching his eyes. "You don't see me as weak?"

"How could I?" Silver Feather said, embracing her and holding her close. "My wife, I should have known you could not do this. I am sorry."

"I'm so glad you understand," Diana said, clinging to him. "Please let's go. I've had enough of being the Goddess of the Hunt. I am your wife. That's all I want to be—except when I become a mother to our children."

"Since we are out here, there is something I want to show you," Silver Feather said, helping her up from the ground. He picked up her rifle and his bow.

They heard a great rustling sound and, looking past the bushes, saw the deer bounding away.

"It is gone now," Silver Feather said, walking with Diana back to the horses.

"But it might be someone else's target very soon," Diana said. "I hope I don't ever disappoint you again."

"My wife, you could never disappoint me," Silver Feather said. He slid her rifle into its gunboot, then helped her into the saddle. "I am proud of you and your good heart. Always remember that."

His bow over his shoulder again, he mounted his white steed.

They rode on until they came to a clearing, then rode across a wide stretch of land.

"Where are you taking me?" Diana asked, gazing over at him, her heart light once again.

"We are there," Silver Feather said, nodding toward a great mound that stood on the ridge of land directly before them.

"What is it?" Diana asked, as they drew a tight rein at the foot of the mound.

"There are many of these large mounds scattered across Indian territory in Mississippi land," Silver Feather said, dismounting.

He helped Diana down from her saddle, then took her hand. They went and stood near the mound, gazing up at it.

"But, my wife, this mound is the most important of them all," he said, pride in his eyes.

"What sort of mound is this?" Diana asked, awed by its hugeness. "Who made it?"

"My Choctaw ancestors," Silver Feather said, walking slowly with Diana around the foot of the mound. "This mound is called Nanih Waiya. For the Choctaw, there is no more important place on earth."

"I don't understand," Diana said.

"I shall try to explain, yet sometimes an explanation is not enough. There is still much about such mounds that is a mystery even to today's Choctaw," Silver Feather said. He stopped, Diana close at his side. "But I will tell you what I can.

"As is told by my people's storytellers, in the ancient past Nanih Waiya gave birth to the

Choctaw. Out of the subterranean womb of the Great Mother Earth crawled the 'beloved people,' and they lay on their bellies to dry themselves in the warm rays of their Great Father, ABA, the sun. Afterward, ABA promulgated his law. He divided the Choctaw into two great families, or *iksas*, and established the social conventions and rituals whereby the new people would enjoy a secure and prosperous existence on earth."

He paused and turned to his wife. Diana listened raptly. Her interest was revealed in her eyes. Silver Feather continued.

"Before returning to his home in the sky, ABA kindled a 'Sacred Fire' that he left burning in his stead as an earthly reminder of 'His Power.' The sun had chosen the Choctaw as his people, and the land around these mounds as their world, and so long as the Choctaw followed his law, they would remain on the bright path to a righteous life. Should they stray from the path and follow the dark one, the monsters who haunted the boundaries of their world would invade their land, bringing destruction and despair."

"The monsters being the white people?" Diana asked, feeling ashamed that her own skin was white.

"Yes," Silver Feather answered thickly. "And so it seems some of my ancestors strayed from the bright path, which caused the invaders to come and take so much of our land."

"I'm sorry," Diana murmured. She stepped into his arms. "As your wife, I shall do everything in my power to make it up to you. We—you and I—lived it, Silver Feather. We saw how my stepfather took so much from your people."

"But that was then. This is now," Silver Feather said, placing his hands on her shoulders and holding her away from him so that their eyes could meet. "I am now my people's leader. I will never follow the dark path."

"Let's go home," Diana said. "We've so much to do to get ready for the big move."

"Yes, the big move," Silver Feather said, walking with her to the horses. He smiled at her. "And soon the Eagle Clan bone house will be rebuilt. My Eagle Clan's world will be whole again."

Diana smiled and nodded.

After she mounted her steed and they began riding away, she looked over her shoulder at the mound. Yes, she had much to learn about her husband's people, but a lifetime in which to learn it.

Chapter 33

I could not love thee, dear, so much
Lov'd I not honor more.
                    —Richard Lovelace

Several lovely bald eagles swept down from the heavens. They seemed like a sign to the Choctaw people who gazed up at them. They watched the magnificent birds soar for a while, appearing and disappearing amid the clouds like hallucinations, then finally vanishing into the billowing white clouds.

Diana stood beside Silver Feather before the newly constructed sacred bone house. Boxes made of cane were being carried, one by one, into the bone house for their final interment.

Diana slid a hand into Silver Feather's and stood proudly at his side. Everything was finally falling into its rightful place.

After Silver Feather's people returned to the land and cleared it of rubble and weeds, several unmarked graves had been found at the far back of the estate grounds.

Through the years, Carolina jessamine vines, now twisted and flowerless, had grown over the graves, making it impossible to recognize them.

The graves had been found by several of Silver Feather's warriors, White Cloud among them, and he had rushed to Silver Feather with the news.

Silver Feather had never known of blacks being used as slaves at the plantation, so he could only surmise that these graves were those of his Choctaw people.

With a heavy heart, Silver Feather removed the dirt from the graves, finding two that he knew immediately were his mother's and father's.

He recognized the clothes they had worn that day, especially his father, who always wore a necklace that proved his chieftainship, although the title had been denied him once he had been forced to work at Dettro Plantation. His father had kept the necklace hidden beneath his shirt, for if he hadn't, it would have been yanked from around his neck and thrown away.

The thin strip of leather upon which a silver medallion hung had rotted, yet the symbol of the eagle against silver was still recognizable.

Silver Feather wore a replica of the necklace on a silver chain even now as he gave his parents their final resting place, this time forever.

Diana could feel Silver Feather's emotions, which were mixed. There was pride in his eyes, yet sadness because the previous bone house had been destroyed and because he had found his parents' bodies.

As more and more boxes were carried into the sacred bone house, Diana thought about Silver Feather's explanation of how his people had come to use bone houses.

He had told her that even back to the earliest of time, the Choctaw had not buried their dead in the ground. They had constructed a wooden scaffold twelve to fifteen feet tall directly opposite the door of the home of the person who had died.

The body had been laid out atop the scaffold, covered with a blanket, and allowed to decompose. When the body was sufficiently rotted, bone pickers took it down, for it had finally passed from life to death. While the spirit journeyed to the afterlife, bone pickers stripped the decayed flesh from the bones with fingernails grown long especially for the task.

They then threw the fetid remains into a sacred fire, painted the skull red, bundled the bones in a box made of cane, and presented the package to the dead's clan for interment in the town bone house.

Afterward, a great feast would be held.

Today, though, the Choctaw no longer practiced such things. When their kin died, they were placed in the ground, and their graves were marked.

Back where the Turtle Clan's village had originally been, there was a burial ground, which was even now being guarded against grave robbers. No one would ever be able to steal from the Choctaw again, and if they tried, they would not live to tell about it.

Finally, the last cane box was taken inside the sacred bone house. Those who had taken it there came out and slowly, meditatively, closed the door, and locked it with a key and chain to protect the house's contents.

And now, just as in the past, great cook fires stretched out across land where cotton had once grown. Huge copper pots sat amid the glowing embers of the fires, sending off tantalizing aromas of various foods. Great slabs of meat turned slowly on spits over the fires, for the warriors' hunt had been successful.

Children were already breaking away from their parents and running to where they knew the feast would take place. Blankets had been spread out on the ground, each family having marked their space before they went to the interment.

Drums were set up, waiting to be played for the celebration, and dancers were gathering just as Diana and Silver Feather reached their blanket and sat down. The women dancers started dancing immediately, in time with the music of the drums, flutes, and rattles. Their skirts were made of feathers that were dyed many different colors, flashing and shimmering as the women's bare feet danced, their faces radiant with smiles as the sun poured its golden light down upon them.

"It is done," Diana said quietly to Silver Feather, smiling a thank-you to a woman who brought two large platters of foods to Diana and Silver Feather.

She recognized corn prepared in many different ways, and deer meat, causing her to recall that day when she could not kill a deer while on the hunt.

"Yes, it is done, and now we can proceed with life as it should have been long ago," Silver Feather said, plucking a piece of meat between his fingers. He took a bite, chewed, then smiled at Diana as he swallowed it.

"We shall make this land profitable," he said proudly. "I envision field after field of cotton, corn, and all other garden foods we Choctaw enjoy eating."

Diana could not help but giggle. "Lately I seem to be eating all the time."

Her eyes beaming, Diana took one of Silver Feather's hands and laid it across her stomach. "My husband, Pretty Fawn and White Cloud's child is going to have a playmate," she said, seeing the pride that leaped quickly into his eyes. "Yes, my husband, I have missed more than one monthly flow now. I am with child. We are going to be parents!"

Silver Feather was momentarily at a loss for

words, then he stood up quickly, leaned down, and swept her into his arms. He carried her through the crowd of Choctaw who were sitting and enjoying their feast and the music and dancers.

But when Silver Feather stepped amid them with his wife in his arms, everyone stopped and stared questioningly at him.

"My people, there is something else for us to rejoice about!" he cried. "Your chief's wife is with child!"

Laughing joyously amid the applause and shouts of congratulation, Silver Feather spun around with Diana, her golden hair flying in the wind, her eyes brimming with happy tears. She had always known that he wanted children. But never had she expected him to be this exuberant.

Oh, what a wonderful father he would be! Their children would never want for love. They would have all they needed, and more.

"Silver Feather, I am getting dizzy," Diana said, clinging to his neck, sighing with relief when he finally stopped, yet still held her in his arms, his eyes gazing with such intensity into hers.

"My wife, you never cease to amaze me," Silver Feather said incredulously. "How can you continue to give me so much? I am grateful, Diana, so very, very grateful to have found you. I love you, Diana. I love you so much."

"And I love you more," she murmured, then

brushed soft kisses across his lips. "I do, my love. Oh, I do."

"I hope that I did not make you too dizzy," Silver Feather said, setting her feet on the ground. "For the moment I forgot everything but how happy and proud that I was."

He gazed down at her stomach and placed a gentle hand on it. "Did I possibly harm the child?"

"No," Diana said, laughing softly. "It would take more than a few spins in your arms to harm our child. My days of being your Goddess of the Hunt are over, however. I don't dare ride a horse anymore. I don't want to take any chances. This child means everything to me."

"To us," Silver Feather quickly corrected her. "But you said something that was not quite true."

"I did?" Diana said, her eyes widening as she gazed into his. "What did I say that wasn't true?"

"You are still a goddess," he said, his eyes gleaming. "Mine."

Diana laughed softly again, then walked with him back to their blanket, where they sat down and continued to enjoy the feast. They watched the children at play as the boys and girls ran around chasing one another and some smaller girls carried their little homemade dolls to where they could play house near a stand of lovely flowering plants.

Past them and the fields that would soon be planted with cotton stood newly built cabins of all sizes alongside a creek that ran behind where Dettro Manor had once stood. Smoke spiraled lazily from the chimneys, where home fires burned in the grates of the fireplaces during these cooler days of autumn.

It was a new beginning, and Diana felt as though she had never been apart from Silver Feather.

She turned to him. "Thank you, darling," she said.

"What is that thank-you for?" he asked, chuckling, for she seemed to be thanking him all the time for something.

"Just for being you," she answered, smiling into his eyes.

Two Winds, the storyteller, came to sit amid the people. "I will tell you why our sight fails with age," he said in his deep, resonant voice. "It begins like this . . . Chickadee-dee-dee-dee, chickadee-dee-dee-dee. 'Oh, he almost came inside the lodge, Grandfather!' cried Bluebird, as a chickadee flew to a bush near the door. 'I like the chickadees. They are always so friendly and happy. I pretend they are laughing when they are in the willows and the rosebushes. They do seem to be laughing, don't they, Grandfather?' 'Yes,' War Eagle said. 'That is what Old-man thought one day long ago. It made trouble for us all, too—bad trouble that visits us if we live to be old.' "

The tale went on and on. Diana listened closely, enchanted by these people and their ways.

She felt Silver Feather's hand slide into hers.

She squeezed it lovingly, still watching and listening to the storyteller.

Epilogue

On this green bank, by this soft stream,
We sat today, a votive stone;
That memory may their deed redeem.
—Ralph Waldo Emerson

Diana sat with Silver Feather as their four-year-old son, Lone Feather, splashed in the stream that ran behind their house. Beyond, beautiful egrets and herons glided gracefully through the cypress trees.

They sat where they could also look out upon the great expanse of cotton fields. As far as the eye could see, the bolls of cotton hung heavy on their plants and were even now being harvested by white people that the Choctaw had hired to do the work that the Choctaw people did not have time for themselves.

The Choctaw had their other personal gardens to tend to, as well as the hunt.

Chance Duffy, the sheriff who had taken in those responsible for turning bones into buttons and combs, was now the overseer who saw that those who worked for the Choctaw did not lapse in their duties.

The rich alluvial soil of the Choctaw land was ideal for the large-scale cotton cultivation that had become the region's staple. There were yields of two to three bales of cotton per acre, and advances in ginning technology and improvements in cotton strains made it even more profitable for those who owned the great fields of cotton plants.

"This year there is an even more abundant cotton crop than last year," Diana commented, as Lone Feather splashed out of the water and raced to her, leaping into her arms and soaking her doeskin dress.

She giggled and held him on her lap as Silver Feather dried him with a soft cloth.

"And each year it will get better and better," Silver Feather said, taking Lone Feather onto his own lap as Diana dressed him in his tiny outfit of fringed buckskin.

She combed her fingers through his thick crop of black hair, then playfully swatted him on his behind before he ran off to join the other children.

She loved to see how his tiny legs could carry him so fast and how his copper skin wore a smooth sheen as the sun's rays fell along it.

"He is you," Diana said, reaching to take Silver Feather's hand. "He is an exact replica of you, and I am so glad."

"But he has the eyes of his mother," Silver Feather said, running his fingers through Diana's long, golden hair.

"He is so content," Diana said, watching Lone Feather chase and laugh with the other children his age, among them Pretty Fawn and White Cloud's son, White Deer.

"He will never have trials of childhood such as we had to go through," Silver Feather said, gathering Diana in his arms and holding her close. "We will see to that."

"Yes, we will give him the peace of mind we never had," Diana murmured.

She watched far beyond the children as Chance Duffy walked slowly among the laborers plucking cotton and placing it in large gunnysacks.

It gave her a feeling of pride to see that some people looked past the color of the Choctaw people's skin instead of looking down on them as though they were just worthless creatures.

These Choctaw had more money than most whites, and as Harry Braddock had once said, money made things happen.

"I must go into council," Silver Feather said, rising and reaching down to help Diana to her feet. He hugged her and said, "I think I smell something delicious cooking on your cookstove."

"Yes, I have finally mastered the art of cooking," Diana said, laughing softly.

She walked with him to their cabin, then stood at the doorway and watched him walk away, toward the great council house that stood in the middle of their village, where Dettro Manor had once stood.

Diana smiled contentedly, then hurried inside to her kitchen, where she had left a peach pie baking in the oven.

As she pulled it free, steam spiraled from the holes she had poked in the crust to enable the heat to escape. She smiled. Yes, she did know how to cook now, just as she knew every other way to be a perfect wife for her husband.

"And it's a labor of love," she whispered, placing the pie on the windowsill to cool.

She looked out the window toward the large expanse of cotton fields, then at the council house where her husband presided over a meeting, and felt a contentment she had never known before.

Yes, it had all come together for them both. Life was what one made of it, and against all odds she and Silver Feather had made a perfect life together.

Happy, she went to her bedroom and ran her hand over the velveteen patchwork quilt that lay across the bed. "Mama, if only you were here to see my happiness," she whispered. "To share it!"

A soft breeze wafted through the open window above the bed, brushing against Diana's cheeks. She smiled, for she could not help but believe that somehow she had just been visited by her beloved mother.

"You do know of my happiness, don't you?" she

whispered, touching her face. "You are here, aren't you, Mama?"

Again she felt the breeze against her cheeks, soft and caressing . . .

Letter to the Reader

Dear Reader:

I hope you enjoyed reading *Silver Feather*. The next book in my Signet Indian series that I am writing exclusively for Signet is *Swift Horse*, about the Creek tribe. *Swift Horse* is filled with much excitement, romance, and adventure!

Those of you who are collecting my Indian novels and want to hear more about my entire backlist of these books, as well as my fan club, can send for my latest newsletter and an autographed bookmark.

Write to:

Cassie Edwards
6709 North Country Club Road
Mattoon, IL 61938

You can also visit my Web site at:
www.cassieedwards.com.

Thank you for your support of my Indian romances. I love researching and writing about our country's first people!

Always,
Cassie Edwards

New York Times bestselling author

Madeline Baker

Under Apache Skies

0-451-21282-7

When a rugged stranger darkens the door of her family
porch, Martha Jean Flynn can tell right away that Ridge
Longtree is nothing like the other cowboys who usually
show up in search of work. But when tragedy strikes,
Marty must flee with the half-Indian loner—and she
discovers a love that threatens to set her heart aflame.

Coming October 2005:

Dakota Dreams

0-451-21686-5

Nathan Chasing Elk was looking for his lost daughter—
and to avenge the death of his wife. Catharine Lyons was
struggling to maintain her ranch when Nathan stumbled
onto her property, badly injured. Together they would
try to mend their lives—and discover a passion neither
has ever known.

**Available wherever books are sold or at
www.penguin.com**

Sweeping prehistoric fables from
New York Times bestselling author

LINDA LAY SHULER

LET THE DRUM SPEAK   190955
Possessed with the same mystical powers as her mother, a young
woman follows her wandering mate to a fabled city in the
prehistoric Southwest. But here her beauty attracts the attention of
the city's supreme ruler—a man who will become her greatest
enemy. Far from her homeland, she must now struggle for her own
survival...and that of her only child.

SHE WHO REMEMBERS   160533
"Linda Lay Shuler....has brought to life the story of the Mesa Verde
and Chaco Canyon, and the ancient people who built those
mysterious hidden canyon cities. I admire her accurate research, but
I loved her compelling story of love and adventure even more."
                    —Jean M. Auel, author of *The Clan of the Cave Bear*

VOICE OF THE EAGLE   176812
Spanning ten years, this magnificent novel, rich in detail, gives an
intimate portrait of a strong and independent woman, who is also
the spiritual leader of her people. Set in the Southwest, this
enthralling tale brings to life the vanished ways of the
first Americans.

Available wherever books are sold at
www.penguin.com